MY SECRET LOVE

When Tamara Cameron's modelling career is cut short after she suffers an injury to her back, she runs a private catering business, relieved to be out of the media spotlight at a time of personal difficulty. But then, scatty Phyllis Morton appears on her doorstep and Tamara's life begins to lurch from one crisis to another, as Phyllis turns out to be the great aunt of Adam Penrose — a man whose marriage proposal she turned down years ago.

MARGARET MOUNSDON

MY SECRET LOVE

Complete and Unabridged

LINFORD
Leicester

First published in Great Britain in 2011

First Linford Edition
published 2012

British Library CIP Data

Mounsdon, Margaret.
   My secret love. - -
   (Linford romance library)
   1. Love stories.
   2. Large type books.
   I. Title II. Series
   823.9'2–dc23

   ISBN 978–1–4448–1254–1

Published by
F. A. Thorpe (Publishing)
Anstey, Leicestershire

Set by Words & Graphics Ltd.
Anstey, Leicestershire
Printed and bound in Great Britain by
T. J. International Ltd., Padstow, Cornwall

This book is printed on acid-free paper

An Unexpected Guest

'Could I use your phone and the facilities, please?' A tall, elegant woman was hopping around on Tamara's front doorstep clad in a vast number of floaty scarves. Their peacock colours attracted the bright sunshine giving her the appearance of an exotic bird of paradise. 'Actually, could I have the comfort break first?'

'Sorry?' Tamara's heartbeat was still going at a rapid pace. The explosion and the smell of hot oil on her forecourt had her leaping to her feet and racing for the door. She looked at the smouldering heap of machinery on her forecourt then back to the agitated woman.

'I'm so sorry to disturb you, dear. I know I am being the most tremendous nuisance, but my old boneshaker has broken down outside your delightful barn, as you can see.' She waved an arm in the direction of the disaster.

'Yes, I can.' Tamara agreed with her on that one.

'Actually, I think it might have run out of something important, oil or water, I'm not sure which. I always forget to check things.'

Tamara hoped this woman wasn't a new customer. She had encountered some pretty unconventional types since she had started up her catering business, but this woman outdid them all.

'It's this way, isn't it?'

Tamara continued to gape as the imposing figure swept past her and made her way towards the bathroom.

'Yes, it is,' she said in a faint voice, then mindful of her position as a dutiful, if reluctant hostess, added, 'You'll find plenty of soap and towels.'

'Thank you, dear.'

She turned back to look at the forecourt. Abandoned on her newly paved parking area was a car of indeterminate age and colour. Its driver-door was hanging open and from its rather perilous angle, it looked as though the vehicle had slewed to a halt in a hurry. Tamara wrinkled her nose. The smell of burning rubber that was caught at the back of her throat and making her cough was no doubt caused by the rapid application of brakes on a wet surface.

The sun breaking through the scudding clouds had now rapidly dispelled an earlier shower, for which Tamara was grateful. She watched the car door sway in the breeze and hoped all four of the vehicle's wheels turned in the same direction and that someone would be able to drive it off her forecourt.

What was a more pressing question was exactly what was the owner doing here?

Bailey's Barn was isolated and quite remote, tucked away down the end of a country lane. That was why Tamara had chosen it. She didn't want photographers dogging her every move, or microphones thrust in her face whenever she went shopping. It had been six months now and she was beginning to hope interest in her story was waning.

Was this woman an undercover reporter? Admittedly she didn't look like one, but who could tell these days? Only yesterday Tamara had been reading of a young woman who had completely changed her appearance for a journalistic assignment. No-one would have believed the bespectacled middle-aged female with wispy hair was actually a blonde, career-orientated twenty-something.

The sound of running tap water alerted Tamara's attention back to the cloakroom.

'Thank you, dear. Too kind.' Her uninvited guest emerged into the hall. 'Now, do you have a telephone I could use?'

'Don't you own a mobile?' Tamara's suspicions were back on full alert. Her number was ex-directory. She still wasn't sure what this woman was doing here, and until she was, her telephone was definitely off limits.

'Can I smell baking?'

'Er, yes,' Tamara replied, temporarily wrong footed by the question.

'You're busy and I've interrupted you. I'm sorry.'

The smell was growing stronger.

'You'd better come into the kitchen,' Tamara issued a reluctant invitation. 'I need to check on the cheese straws.'

'Cheese straws?' The older woman's face lit up. 'My absolute favourite savoury snack. Do you think we could indulge in one with some coffee while I call the garage? Adam is absolutely hopeless at stocking up the fridge so I missed out on breakfast. I haven't had even as much as a cup of tea this morning. That's where I was going, to the supermarket, but Vladimir conked out on me, so here I am.'

Her smile was one of the most beautiful Tamara had seen in a long time. On closer inspection the woman appeared to be older than she had first seemed. She had a relatively unlined face, classic cheekbones and the most magnetic blue eyes. Her silvery hair, untouched by any artificial colour, was arranged in a topknot that looked in danger of disintegrating at any moment.

Tamara poured out two cups of coffee then after checking on the progress of the current batch of cheese straws, produced some from a tin she always kept handy for visitors.

'That's something else I keep forgetting to top up or whatever it is you're supposed to do,' her uninvited guest explained, through delicate bites of cheese straw. 'These are to die for,' she said, closing her eyes in ecstasy. 'You should be a professional cook.'

'I am.'

'Are you really?'

'What do you keep forgetting to top up?' Tamara asked, having difficulty keeping up with the flow of the conversation.

'The credit on my mobile phone. I'm Phyllis Morton, by the way. I should have introduced myself earlier. I do apologise.'

'Tamara Cameron.'

They shook hands while Tamara held her breath waiting to see if the woman recognised her.

'What a pretty name.'

It was obvious from her expression she didn't.

'It's Cornish.'

'Surely Cameron's Scottish, isn't it?'

'My mother came from St Ives.'

'Another lovely part of the world. Full of artists and cobbled streets.'

'You know it?'

'I spent several lovely holidays there with a certain gentleman friend, many years ago.' A dreamy look came into Phyllis's blue eyes. 'He was so romantic. He had fresh flowers delivered to my room every day.'

Outside, the May morning was now getting into full swing. It had blown away the rain and the garden shone in the sunshine. The blossom on the apple tree swayed in the breeze, and the scent of newly mown grass wafted through the open window.

'I love this time of year, don't you?' Phyllis returning to more practical matters helped herself to a second cheese straw. 'You don't mind?'

'Yes, I do, and no, I don't mind.' Tamara answered both questions.

'Are you cooking for a party?'

'A finger buffet.'

'I suppose I should offer to help. You don't need any help, do you?' Phyllis's offer did not sound too enthusiastic.

'What sort of help?' Tamara asked.

'I don't know.' Phyllis shrugged. 'A washer upper, delivery girl, that sort of thing? Something to pay you back for me being a nuisance.'

Tamara thought of the car abandoned on her forecourt and decided to decline the offer.

'I've got my own transport, thank you, and I use a dishwasher.'

Phyllis didn't look in the least upset by the put down. 'You've probably made a wise decision. I'm not the most reliable of people.'

'Do you live nearby?' Tamara asked.

'Actually, I used to live here.'

'In Hayminster?'

The wilds of deepest Kent did not look like the natural habitat of Phyllis Morton. Someone possessing her Slavic beauty would have looked more at home in one of the capital cities of Eastern Europe.

'No, here, I used to live in Bailey's Barn.'

'What?'

'As a tenant. I didn't own it and it didn't look quite as lovely as it does now. You've done well,' Phyllis said with a nod of approval. 'It's not too fussy and you haven't townified it. Is that a word? Anyway,' she beamed at Tamara, 'I like it. I do hope we'll be friends too. I usually make up my mind about people very quickly and I think you and I are twin souls.'

'Yes,' Tamara replied, not sure exactly what she was agreeing to, but unable to think of anything else to say.

'I'm staying over with my great-nephew for a few days. He's got one of those converted warehouses down by the river. Do you know where I mean?'

'On Waterman's Wharf?' Tamara asked.

There had been pages about it in the local press and a lot of opposition. The warehouses were a bit of a landmark and many people wanted them to remain as they were. Privately Tamara thought they were a bit of an eyesore. She was one of the few who had welcomed the development.

'That's the place. What do you think of it?'

'It's an expensive place to live.'

'And full of yuppies. Not my scene really, but my great-nephew likes it. He's one for wide-open spaces and he's got huge windows that let in the morning light and the view over the estuary is stunning. He's on sick leave at the moment, so I keep dropping in to keep an eye on him.'

'What exactly does he do?'

'Adam? He's a journalist.'

Tamara stiffened as her cheese straw churned in her stomach. Her suspicions had been correct. All this 'my car has broken down act', was exactly that, an act. By very clever, devious means, Phyllis had wormed her way into Tamara's house. It was a bitter pill to swallow.

Tamara had been beginning to like the older woman. She took a deep breath, ready to tell Phyllis exactly what she thought of her underhand tactics, but before she could speak, Phyllis asked, 'Would you mind if I used your telephone, dear? I know it's an awful cheek, but if I don't you're going to be stuck with me forever. I can quite understand your not trusting me, after all, why should you? But I assure you I'm not about to case the joint. I've never stolen a thing in my life.'

Phyllis's blinding smile made Tamara squirm. Had her suspicions been reflected on her face? Phyllis scratched around in her voluminous shoulder bag before producing a creased business card.

'Here's the number of the garage. Would you like to dial it for me? I'm not sure where I've left my glasses.'

Moments later Phyllis was connected to her garage.

'Well, really.' She slammed down the receiver after a heated exchange, involving much arm waving and raising of her voice.

'Is there a problem?' Tamara asked.

'They say there's nothing more they can do for Vladimir and that they told me so last time he went in for a service.'

Tamara wanted to laugh at the look of outrage on Phyllis's face.

'And did they? I take it Vladimir is your car?'

'Yes, and they did. They tried to sell me a new one, implying Vladimir was ready for the scrap heap.' Phyllis was now well and truly in her stride. 'But I've never in my life listened to anything men have to say. They waffle on dreadfully about things I don't understand.'

The blue eyes widened in dramatic indignation.

'Perhaps you should have done this time — listened to a man? They do occasionally make sense.' The ghost of a smile softened Tamara's lips before she remembered she was now stuck with an uninvited houseguest.

'I don't intend to change the habit of a lifetime. What's that strange noise?' Phyllis asked looking round as a buzzing rent the air.

'I rather think it's your mobile phone. The one you said had run out of credit.'

'Good heavens,' Phyllis retrieved it from her handbag. 'It's actually working.' She stared at it in amazement as a number flashed up.

'Don't you think you ought to answer it?' Tamara had great difficulty keeping the renewed scepticism out of her voice.

'Would you be an angel and answer it for me?' Phyllis asked.

'Why?'

Phyllis pressed the green button then lowered her voice. 'It's my great-nephew, Adam.'

'You don't want to speak to him?'

'He's another one who will lecture me. Tell him I'm out.'

'How can you be out when you're on the other end of a mobile phone?' Tamara hissed back.

'Hello?' An irate male voice called out down the other end of the line.

'Oh, hello,' Tamara replied, wondering what on earth she was going to say.

'Who's that?' the man demanded.

'Er, are you Adam?' Tamara asked tentatively.

'Where's my great-aunt? What are you doing answering her telephone? She hasn't been in an accident has she?'

Phyllis was busy shaking her head and flapping her hands at Tamara, a look of panic on her face.

'He gets so grumpy when this happens,' she mouthed, 'I'm sure you can sweet talk him out of his bad mood.'

'You mean you make a habit of breaking down on people's forecourts?'

'It happens all the time,' Phyllis

replied in wide-eyed surprise as if she couldn't believe why.

'If she's told you she's out, you can tell her from me, I don't believe her. She tried to play that trick on me last time.'

'No, she's not out actually. She's here,' Tamara admitted, 'and she's perfectly all right. She hasn't been injured or anything like that.'

It was useless pretending otherwise as both she and Phyllis had forgotten to whisper and Adam must have heard every word of their latest exchange.

'Look, I know you're not going to believe this, er, Adam,' Tamara tried to explain, 'but she broke down on my forecourt.'

'Now there you're wrong.' There was weary acceptance in Adam's voice. 'I do believe you.'

'She needed to use my, um, facilities, so I invited her in. Then we had a cup of coffee and some cheese straws.'

'Where do you live?'

'I'll make myself scarce,' Phyllis said

making a thumbs up sign at Tamara, 'need a breath of fresh air.' She eased open her back door and sidled onto the terrace.

'Bailey's Barn,' Tamara said.

'Isn't that where she used to live?' Adam asked.

'Yes,' Tamara replied, relieved that at least one part of Phyllis's story was true. It was important to remember this Adam was a journalist.

'Your great-aunt has already telephoned the garage.'

'With little success, I should imagine.'

'I'm afraid so,' Tamara admitted. 'Does she do this sort of thing often?'

'It's not unknown. Last time she broke down it was outside a monastery and the chap in charge very wisely wouldn't let her in. He played the men only here rule.'

A bubble of reluctant laughter rose in Tamara's chest.

'Look, sorry, I don't know your name?'

'Tamara Cameron,' she replied.

There was a telling silence down the line.

'Hello? Are you still there?' Tamara asked.

'Is this some kind of joke?' Adam demanded.

'I'm sorry,' Tamara frowned. 'I don't understand.'

'Are you *the* Tamara Cameron?'

Tamara's heart sank. For the moment she had completely forgotten her minor celebrity status and the scandal that had been dogging her footsteps for the last six months.

'Yes,' she admitted.

'And you're living at Bailey's Barn?'

Furious with herself for so indiscreetly revealing her address, Tamara could only agree again.

'So you've finally wound up back here. What a coincidence.'

'Sorry?' Tamara frowned in confusion, not following the trend of his comment.

'What goes round comes round.'

Tamara began to suspect Adam

17

might be as peculiar as his great-aunt. Neither of them seemed to make much sense.

'You're going to have to run that past me again.'

'I'm talking about you and me.'

'What?' Tamara asked in a faint voice.

'Adam Penrose. Ring any bells?'

Phyllis's mobile almost slipped from Tamara's fingers.

'You're Phyllis's great-nephew?'

'Yes.'

Tamara swayed and grabbed the wall for support.

'Are you still there?'

'Yes, I am. Hello, Adam,' Tamara said in a shaky voice.

'Is that all you can say?'

'Yes.'

Tamara's cover was now well and truly blown. Adam Penrose was one of the leading journalists of the day and the last time she had seen him was when she had told him she couldn't marry him because she was in love with Myles Johnson.

A Voice From The Past

'I should have thought using your great aunt to do your dirty work was a little too low even for you.' Tamara squared her shoulders, determined to get her shot in first.

'What exactly do you mean by that remark?' Adam demanded, sounding equally angry.

'You've been commissioned to do a piece on me, haven't you?'

'I don't know what you're talking about.'

'Realising you had a connection with the woman everyone wants to interview was too great a temptation for you to ignore, I suppose?'

'Interviewing pampered supermodels who won't get out of bed unless they are paid an exorbitant fee is hardly my scene and you know it.'

Tamara could hear the outrage in

Adam's voice. She bit her lip. What he said was true. Adam's field of expertise was at the grittier end of journalism. He had travelled all over the world and he wasn't afraid to be hands on when it came to in depth reporting.

An apology hovered on Tamara's lips, before Adam added, 'Modelling is for lightweights and I don't do lightweight work.'

'Modelling is hard work,' Tamara retaliated. 'You try getting up at all hours, standing around for ages in cotton dresses in freezing muddy fields or sweltering in boiling sunshine wearing winter woollies and trying to smile at the same time. I've had to dangle off builders' scaffolding for an exclusive shot and once I even had to pose in a Spanish bull ring, with the bull, so let me tell you it's not all big ticket contracts.'

Tamara's protest fell on deaf ears.

'And to suggest I'd use my great-aunt for my purposes is way out of order.'

Why hadn't she recognised Adam's

voice earlier? Tamara pushed her hair off her face, her thoughts in turmoil. She had never really recovered from her feeling of remorse over what had happened between them. She thought they had never been that serious an item and she'd had no idea Adam had intended proposing, the night she told him about Myles.

She took a deep breath endeavouring to forget the personal baggage between them before asking in as controlled a voice as she could manage, 'Then can you explain what Phyllis is doing on my doorstep?'

'Try asking her.' Adam's response was a pithy one liner.

'I have, but I don't seem to be getting anywhere.'

Tamara tweaked back the curtain. There was no sign of Phyllis. She would appear, very wisely to have gone to ground, and Tamara didn't blame her. With Adam as a great nephew, she would probably have done the same.

'Hmm, know the feeling. Where is she now?'

'She's gone for a walk in the garden,' Tamara explained.

Adam's voice lost some of its fire. 'To give Phyllis her due, she doesn't fib. It's her way of saying she's out. She's probably reacquainting herself with the grounds. The flowerbeds were her pride and joy.'

'I had no idea she used to live here.'

'It broke her heart when she had to leave. I would have bought the barn for her, but I was away on an assignment at the time and by the time I came back, the sale had gone through.'

'The late owner's son lives abroad and in order to wind up her estate he wanted a quick deal,' Tamara explained.

'I never dreamed you were the purchaser.'

'For once I was in the right place at the right time, I suppose.' Tamara paused.

During her brief relationship with Adam she had grown to love this part of the world and that was why she had chosen to move back here. She had been foolish not to realise Adam could still be in the vicinity. In her day he had rented a cottage, but from what Phyllis had told her Adam too had purchased his own property.

'I'm sorry, Adam, for everything,' Tamara forced out her apology.

She held her breath as silence fell between them.

'How are you?' Adam asked eventually.

Tamara gripped her handset. Adam was media savvy and from the gentler tone of his voice it was obvious he knew all about Myles.

'Bearing up,' she said, injecting an upbeat note into her voice. Right now her defences weren't at their most robust.

'Really?' Adam sounded unconvinced.

'No,' Tamara shook her head. She had never been able to hoodwink him. 'To be honest the last few months have been the pits.'

'Myles Johnson?'

'Partly,' Tamara admitted.

'I'd like to strangle him.'

Tamara swallowed the blockage in her throat.

'It wasn't his fault his business folded,' Tamara insisted, 'and it wouldn't have made the headlines if so many celebrities hadn't been involved. He's working hard to pay back every penny.'

'You always were quick to run to his defence, weren't you?' There was now a trace of a sneer in Adam's voice.

'He didn't do anything wrong. Market forces were against him.'

'I'm not talking about his holiday venture. That could have happened to anyone. I'm talking about your personal life.'

'Which is none of your business.'

'If you call ditching your loyal girlfriend for Jasmine Fenwick, the spoilt daughter of Bob Fenwick and someone who has never done a day's work in her life, is doing nothing wrong, then clearly we have different standards.'

It was something Tamara had gone over in her head day after day. It was the reason she had stepped the wrong way off the catwalk and hurt her back, effectively ending her modelling career. She had been thinking about Myles and Jasmine. He'd told Tamara it had been love at first sight.

Tamara couldn't help thinking it was more a case of Jasmine's father having enough money to settle all Myles's debts, whereas Tamara's father was an impoverished, if happy, artist, but Tamara's loyalty to Myles forbade her from trashing him to Adam.

'It's all water under the bridge now. I've moved on and I'm pleased for him and Jasmine,' she insisted.

Adam made a non-committal noise at the back of his throat.

'I read about your accident online.'

'That was something else the press blew up out of all proportion.'

Tamara felt sick as she remembered

some of the more sensational headlines. One reporter, whom she'd never even met, had written a story, saying she'd told him she'd fallen off the catwalk on purpose in an attempt to win Myles back.

'What really happened?' Adam asked.

'I hurt my back because I stepped off the catwalk. I wasn't looking where I was going and it was totally my fault. Period. I've got a good physiotherapist who's given me a list of exercises to do and these days the injury hardly bothers me at all.'

'And Myles?'

'I haven't seen him since I moved in here.'

'How did you end up in Bailey's Barn?' Adam sounded slightly more mollified.

'I had been half heartedly looking for something in this area for a while.'

'Happy memories?' Adam asked in a wry voice.

'It was my agent who saw the advertisement and she told me about it when it came on the market, so I viewed it and we exchanged contracts within the month. It seemed an ideal place for setting up my own business.'

'Doing what?' Adam asked.

'Catering.'

'What sort of catering?' Adam could hardly disguise his disbelief.

'Finger buffets, wedding receptions, children's parties, anything, really.'

'You can't cook.'

'There's a lot of things I've had to learn to do recently,' Tamara said in a quiet voice.

'I suppose so,' Adam agreed. 'You learn who your friends are when your luck runs out, don't you?'

Something niggled at the back of Tamara's mind.

'Did I understand Phyllis to say you were on sick leave?' she asked.

When they had been together, it had been one of her greatest fears that Adam would be wounded during the course of his duty. His job was dangerous and whenever he had been away on a mission she'd stayed glued to the satellite news, although watching every bulletin was a nightmare.

'Walking wounded, that's me.'

'It's not serious, is it?' she asked, unable to control the rapid beating of her heart.

'Nothing a few months out of the saddle won't cure.'

Tamara suspected Adam was making light of things.

'What happened? Where were you?' Tamara knew she had no right to feel so anxious, Adam was nothing more than a part of her past, but in a cutthroat profession, he was quite simply one of the nicest most honest people she knew. When he reported a story he had no need to invent falsehoods. He told the truth.

'Chechnya. Took a bullet meant for someone else. You know me. Always in the way.'

'Are you OK?' Tamara gasped.

'I've had better moments, I'll admit,' Adam said, 'but I'm getting there. So,' he laughed, 'we're a couple of old crocks.'

'You always hated not being out in the field. It must be driving you mad not to be in the thick of things.'

'Actually, I've been commissioned to write a book.'

'You don't write fiction.'

'It's not fiction. It's about people who've gone beyond the call of duty in the name of their country. I've done loads of interviews and I've got piles of notes. It's making sense of them that's the challenge.'

'It sounds impressive.'

'Phyllis has been helping me.'

'You're not serious?'

'She was looking for something to do. Every so often she feels the need for a change of scenery and she descends on me.'

'She doesn't live with you all the time?'

'Heaven forbid. She's got a small flat in a church about five miles away. Anyway, what are we going to do about her? I can't drive at the moment.'

'I could drive her over to you, I suppose,' Tamara suggested. 'I've got some deliveries scheduled.'

'You'll do no such thing,' Adam insisted. 'I'll order a taxi.'

'That's not necessary.' Tamara's reply was sharper than she had intended.

'Don't you want to see me again?' Adam taunted her.

His question was too close to the truth for Tamara's peace of mind. The last time they had met, the look on his face had torn at her very soul. She had never been the sort of girl who two-timed men and once she'd realised her relationship with Myles was growing serious, she'd done the decent thing and told Adam. When he had proposed, it was as if the ground had been cut away from beneath her feet. It had been the last thing she suspected. Their worlds could not have been more different and because of their professional lifestyles sometimes they were lucky to meet up once a month.

'It's been a while, hasn't it?' Tamara stalled.

'Two years and six months to be precise.'

'What?' Tamara asked in a faint voice, now awash with guilt.

'Time I got a life, isn't it?' Adam joked.

If she closed her eyes Tamara could see Adam in her mind's eye, sprawled out in a chair behind his desk, his long legs never quite fitting under the flap. He had not been the tidiest of workers.

Papers would bestrew his work surface; piles of photos would constantly slip to the floor; screwed up reports would overflow from the waste paper basket, from where his aim had missed its target. To Tamara's intense annoyance whenever she complained about the state of his study he would challenge her to ask him to find something. In all the time they had been together he had never failed to put his hands on a report or his latest copy.

'Where were you hit?' The question

fell from Tamara's lips, speaking her thoughts out loud.

'I told you, in Chechnya.'

'I meant,' Tamara cleared her throat, 'how bad was it, really?'

'A flesh wound in the shoulder. I'm all strapped up. That's why I can't drive at the moment. At times it hurts like mad and it's not easy putting my socks on, I can tell you. Not still concerned about me, are you?'

'I wouldn't want any harm to come to you,' Tamara replied.

They were treading on dangerous ground. Perhaps it was her conscience, or because she hadn't realised quite how deep her feelings for Adam were, but wherever she was in the world, she still hadn't shaken off the habit of watching the foreign news in the hope of catching a glimpse of him. She rarely did. Adam was a journalist who shunned publicity, but his in-depth investigative reports were accurate and eagerly sought after by all the news channels. He preferred to freelance.

That way he could work to his own schedule and be his own man.

'Now there you and I agree,' he injected a note of lightness into his voice. 'I wouldn't want any harm to come to me, either.' He paused. 'So, back to the business in hand.'

'What? Oh, yes. Phyllis?'

'As I understand the situation, you have one broken-down old banger on your forecourt and my great aunt is loose on the premises?'

'Yes.'

'Right, well I'll make sure she arranges for someone to collect her car, and I'll call for a taxi in about half-an-hour?'

'If you're sure it's not too much trouble?'

'No trouble at all,' Adam replied cheerfully. 'I could do with a breath of fresh air. I was getting restless going through dusty old memoirs, trying to make sense of my notes and Phyllis's scribble. Put the kettle on. I like my coffee black, no sugar.'

Tamara put down the telephone. Seeing Adam again after two and a half years would be a challenge, but she hoped she was adult enough to deal with her emotions. Phyllis's presence would ease any tension and act as a buffer between them.

Tamara strolled onto the terrace, dead-heading a few late daffodils as she enjoyed the feeling of sunshine on her skin. It was something she had never been allowed to do in her modelling days. Her skin freckled easily and the make up artists could never tone them down.

'Phyllis?' she called out. 'Where are you?'

There was no reply. Stifling a sigh of exasperation Tamara descended the steps. As yet she hadn't had much time to attend to the garden and apart from having the lawn mown once a week by a local contractor, she had done very little else. Her fingers itched to get going. She loved the feel of earth under her fingernails and now she no longer needed daily manicures, there was nothing to stop her digging as deep as she liked.

The grounds surrounding Bailey's Barn were not that extensive and a quick five minutes' trawl covered the whole area. Tamara had even peered into the shed suspecting Phyllis might be having a snooze in one of the deckchairs, but there was no trace of her.

This could not be happening Tamara thought as she looked round in exasperation. Phyllis had disappeared.

'It Will Be Like Old Times'

Tamara raced round to the front of the barn. The broken-down car was still on the forecourt. She yanked open the lopsided driver door and looked inside. The foot well was littered with discarded parking tickets, sweet wrappings, shopping receipts, paper bags and a wickerwork shopping basket containing a leather purse.

She picked it up. Surely Phyllis wouldn't have gone off without her purse? Tamara had walked round the garden three times now and done a quick tour of the house in case the older woman had slipped back in while she'd been on the telephone to Adam. There was absolutely no trace of her.

Tamara's lips tightened. She'd had enough of this nonsense. When Adam arrived he was going to be on the receiving end of a few home truths. She couldn't afford to have her time wasted like this. Her business schedule for the day was shot to bits.

Behind her she heard the sound of car tyres rolling down the drive. She turned round, her deep blue eyes steely chips of annoyance. She was more than ready to do battle with Adam Penrose.

As he clambered out of the back seat, it was all Tamara could do to keep a rein on her emotions. In the two-and-a-half years since she had seen him, he had changed, if anything for the better. His chestnut hair was still as spiky and slightly unkempt as it had always been, but there were lines around his eyes that hadn't been there before. On a woman they would have been ageing, but unfair as it was, on Adam they gave him an air of maturity and authority.

He turned to face her, the corner of his mouth quirking into a smile of welcome. His right arm was encased in a sling.

'Hello, Tammy,' he greeted her.

His voice still held a trace of the

Yorkshire accent Tamara so loved. She was glad his years of travelling the world had not honed it down to the semi sophisticated transatlantic twang favoured by many of his colleagues.

'You've put on weight. It suits you. You were far too skinny before. Nice dress.'

His chocolate-brown eyes moved approvingly over the flowered sundress she was wearing. His compliments wrong-footed Tamara. She had been expecting confrontation.

'It's a model,' she said, referring to her dress, then instantly flushed over the foolishness of her remark. Adam had never had much time for fashion. In his world clothes were practical things, things to be worn to keep you warm and decent. Colour, style and cut meant absolutely nothing to him.

'Of course it is,' he agreed solemnly, his lips grazing her cheek in a welcome kiss.

'Since when did you start doing designer stubble?' Tamara demanded, wishing the touch of his flesh on hers didn't make her fingertips tingle.

'Since your telephone call dragged me out of bed,' he replied.

'If I remember correctly, it was you who phoned Phyllis and it was half-past eleven in the morning, hardly the crack of dawn.'

'I had a late night.' Adam stifled a yawn and massaged his injured shoulder.

He was still standing close enough to Tamara for her to feel the heat from his body.

'I thought you'd been injured in the course of duty.'

'I wasn't out on the tiles if that's what you're thinking. I was working if you must know, besides,' he added with what bordered on a rakish smile, 'these days I've no one to go out on the tiles with.'

'Your social life is of no interest to me,' Tamara replied, wondering why Adam found it necessary to let drop that nugget of information.

'Is the coffee ready?' he asked.

'You'd better pay off the taxi,' Tamara clipped back at him. 'I can't find Phyllis.'

The smile drained from Adam's face.

'What do you mean you can't find her?'

'Exactly what I say. She's missing. Not around. Done a runner.'

'Are you sure she's not holed up in a remote corner of the garden?'

'I've looked everywhere. You're welcome to have a try, but I've looked in all the places I can think of.'

'Thanks, Ben.' Adam thrust a note at the taxi driver. 'Keep the change. I'll call you later if I need you.'

'Good luck,' Ben smiled at the pair of them; then, reversing his taxi around Phyllis's abandoned car, drove out of the forecourt.

'You'd better come inside,' Tamara led Adam into the kitchen.

He sat down at the breakfast bar and helped himself from the plate of cheese straws still on the table.

'Here.' Tamara nudged over the basket and purse that she'd picked up off the doorstep. 'They belong to Phyllis and were in the car.'

'These are very good,' Adam waved a cheese straw in the air. 'So you really can cook these days?'

'I did a catering course after my modelling contract expired,' Tamara explained as she poured out fresh coffee, 'and you and Phyllis are doing a great job of eating my profits. Those cheese straws were destined for a finger buffet at the Town Hall.'

'Sorry,' Adam's apology sounded anything but. 'Cheese straws have always been a weakness of mine, and . . . '

'You haven't had any breakfast this morning because the fridge was empty?'

'You've heard the story before?'

'From Phyllis.'

Adam stirred his coffee awkwardly with his left hand.

'Would you like me to pay for His Worship The Mayor's cheese straws?'

he asked. 'I could borrow Phyllis's small change.' He put down his spoon and picked up her purse.

'What exactly is going on, Adam?' Tamara demanded, ignoring his offer.

'Going on?' he raised an eyebrow.

'What is your great-aunt playing at?'

'Not sure,' he admitted, breathing in carefully as if to think things through. 'Phyllis probably forgot she didn't live here any more and strolled off to visit an old friend or something. She has always been a bit forgetful.'

'I'd call it more than forgetful, Adam. What was she doing here in the first place? Bailey's Barn is not on the supermarket route from Waterman's Wharf.'

'Well, no,' Adam agreed, 'it's not.'

'So, for some unknown reason she ends up here. Her car breaks down on my forecourt. She comes in for coffee. Tells me her mobile phone doesn't work. When it miraculously leaps into life and it's you, she sneaks out into the garden and disappears. You can't blame me for wondering what she is doing.'

Adam's slow smile broadened. 'I agree, her behaviour does sound spectacular even by Phyllis's standards.'

'And why aren't you out there scouring the hedgerows looking for her instead of scoffing cheese straws? She may have had an accident, fallen down or something.'

'Because I'd rather sit here, drinking your coffee, scoffing your cheese straws, as you so eloquently put it, and playing catch up with you.'

Tamara's chest heaved as she tried to control her racing breath.

'You don't seem to be taking the situation seriously.'

'That's because Phyllis has done this sort of thing before. I'm sure she'll do it again.'

'What sort of thing?'

'Going out shopping and getting distracted.' Adam made a gesture towards the window. 'It's a lovely day. She meant to go shopping, but then decided she would like to re-visit

Bailey's Barn on her way and introduce herself to the new owner. It's the sort of thing she would do.'

'And then disappear?'

'Like I said, she's probably gone for a walk.'

'Gone for a walk?' Tamara echoed in disbelief. 'Exactly what planet does your great-aunt inhabit?'

'I've often asked myself the very same question,' Adam stretched out his long jean clad legs. 'Don't worry, Tammy.' He used the pet name he'd given her in the past. 'I'm sure nothing serious has happened to her.'

'I wish I shared your optimism.'

'If you like I'll have a look for her later, but right now I'm enjoying my coffee.' Adam looked round the newly fitted kitchen. 'So you live here now.'

'What's that got to do with anything?'

'We're neighbours. We'll be able to drop in on each other. It will be like old times.'

'You mean take up where we left off?' Tamara wasn't sure she could stand many more shocks in one day.

The amusement left Adam's eyes. 'It doesn't do much for a man's ego to be turned down after proposing marriage. I'm not putting myself up for a second dose.'

'If it's any consolation,' Tamara confessed in a quiet voice, 'I know exactly how you must have felt.'

'I take it you are referring to Myles Johnson?'

His name danced in the air between them.

'I didn't know about Jasmine,' Tamara cleared her throat, 'until I saw a picture of them together in one of the gossip mags. He'd told me he was having a boys' weekend.'

'It would appear you let me down a lot lighter.'

Tamara gave a shaky smile.

'Neither was it the experience of a lifetime to have your personal life emblazoned in bold headlines on nearly every newspaper in the land.'

'Do you still love Myles?'

'We meant a lot to each other.'

It still hurt Tamara to remember exactly how much Myles had meant to her.

'That's not a proper answer.'

'It's the only one you're going to get,' Tamara snapped back at him.

Adam put out his left hand and clutched hers across the table. 'Please don't take this the wrong way,' he began.

'Now what?' Tamara demanded.

'You were involved financially with Myles, weren't you?'

'That really is none of your business.'

'You invested heavily in his company and lost most of your money.'

'My financial affairs are private. I'd like you to leave, please.' She snatched her hand away from Adam's.

'I haven't come here to gloat,' Adam insisted, 'or to get a sneaky interview out of you.'

'Then why are you here? You certainly haven't come looking for your lost great-aunt.'

'I've come to offer you help.'

'What sort of help?'

'This book I'm writing.'

'What about it?'

'Could you do with earning some extra money?'

'I thought Phyllis was helping you with it.'

'I'm on a deadline and well.' Adam shrugged. 'You've seen what Phyllis is like. She's got a butterfly mind. Every time I suggest a morning's session, she decides she's got something more interesting to do. Last night I proposed we went through her paperwork to see if we could get it in some sort of order. She wasn't very enthusiastic, to say the least.'

'Her paperwork?'

'There's a reference to Phyllis in my book.'

'Since when did Phyllis give her all for her country?'

'Before she retired she actually had a very interesting career,' Adam said.

'You're not telling me she worked for

the secret service?' Tamara could not keep the disbelief out of her voice.

'Her father was Russian and with her knowledge of the language she was of great help to the authorities.'

'Isn't that sort of thing supposed to remain secret?'

'Certain parts of it, of course, but she and her sister, Irina, my grandmother, were great beauties in their day and they led fascinating lives. I thought a section on them would provide some light relief.'

'Perhaps parts of Phyllis's past are rather more colourful than others and that's why she's reluctant to help you.'

'She wasn't a double agent or anything like that,' Adam insisted.

'I'm only saying, well, like me with Myles, there are areas of your life you'd rather not go into in any depth.'

'I can be trusted to be discreet,' Adam protested.

'Even so, you're not telling me a woman as glamorous as Phyllis hasn't had her fair share of gentlemen friends.

She's still a very vibrant, attractive female.'

'Look, all this is beside the point. Do you want to help me or not?' Adam asked.

Tamara hesitated. When Myles's business had crashed so spectacularly, leaving her and many other investors out of pocket, Tamara hadn't known what to do. At the time she would have leapt at any offer, even Adam's, to make some extra money, but a clever accountant had managed to rework her finances, and over time she had re-invented her career. The thought of working closely with Adam was not one she would relish. Being together in close quarters day after day was not a good idea. Her emotions were still bruised from her relationship with Myles. She was not ready to repeat the experience, but how could she break it gently to Adam?

'Thank you for the offer, but no.' Tamara shook her head.

'You're not interested?' The brown

eyes reflected his surprise.

'Sorry. I've got more than enough to do here. Paperwork was never one of my strengths and I can't type. In fact,' Tamara glanced at the wall clock, 'I really should be getting on with my deliveries. The mayor won't wait forever for his savoury snacks. So if you'll excuse me?'

'And I have wasted enough of my time too this morning being called out on a wild goose chase.'

'What did you say?' His throwaway remark caught Tamara on the hop.

'I have a deadline to meet.'

'I'm equally busy and I did not call you out on a wild goose chase. You offered to come over to collect your great-aunt.'

'It's obvious you misunderstood her intentions.'

'To break down on my forecourt?' Tamara threw back her head, her eyes challenging Adam's. 'You're right. I never saw that one coming.'

With a brisk nod of his head, Adam

stood up. 'I'm sorry she bothered you. It won't happen again.'

'Hang on a moment,' Tamara put out a hand to detain him. Adam looked down to where her fingers were clutching his arm. She flushed and removed her hand.

'Would it be too much to ask of you to let me know exactly what happened to Phyllis if and when she re-appears?'

'Like I say, she's most likely gone to the garage.'

'But they refused to come out to pick up her car.'

'Not your problem,' Adam dismissed her fears firmly, before he began punching a number into his mobile phone.

'Suzie?' He turned his back on Tamara, who, fuming over his rudeness, immediately began to check up on her delivery list. For someone who pretended to have no-one to go out with, Adam was able to conjure up a willing female with remarkable speed. 'Could you be an absolute angel and collect me from Bailey's Barn? What? Yes, 'fraid so, another of Phyllis's scrapes. I'm stuck here without a car. If you're free could you do the honours? Marvellous. I'll see you in about ten minutes.'

'All fixed?' Tamara asked in as polite a manner as she could manage.

'Yes, thank you. I'll be off then. By the way, you've done wonders with the old place, scrubbed pine and state of the art fittings, very nice. Must have cost a lot of cheese straws. I'll see myself out.'

With a quick wave of his hand, Adam was gone.

Tamara heard a car draw up outside a quarter-of-an-hour later and couldn't resist peering through the blinds.

A blindingly beautiful blonde was driving an equally blindingly red sports car. Its paintwork gleamed in the early afternoon sunshine. The driver reminded Tamara of the sort of eager-eyed ingénues who hung around the fashion houses hoping to be spotted by an agent. At twenty-four,

Tamara was considered on the mature side for modelling and she was sure her place had been taken by a similar girl to the one offering Adam a lift.

Tamara was pleased she was no longer a part of that world. The constant competition to look your best was wearing. Lost in her thoughts, she was unaware Adam had glanced up at the window.

Catching sight of her, he waved goodbye with his left hand before easing into the passenger seat. The girl leaned across and flinging her arms around Adam's neck kissed him. From where Tamara was standing, it didn't look as though Adam would have much difficulty, finding a suitable female companion for any further nights out he had planned.

Annoyed with herself for having believed him when he said there was no significant female in his life, she slammed shut her cupboards and began looking round for her own car keys.

A Welcome Visit

'Darling, how wonderful to see you.' Merrill kissed her daughter on both cheeks. 'What a lovely surprise.'

Tamara wallowed in the smell of her mother's signature perfume. It was like no other she had known, a mixture of wild orchid and oil paint. There was no other way to describe it.

'Josh,' she called over her shoulder to her husband, 'our beautiful daughter has crossed the River Tamar. She's home.'

It was a family custom that whenever Tamara wanted to visit her parents she would ring them up and announce she was crossing the Tamar, the river that separated Cornwall from England, the river after which she had been named. Only when she had done that could she really say she saw home.

Morenwyn Cottage was squeezed

into a corner of a cobble-stoned side street, down which cars never ventured. Tamara knew better than to try. She always left her car, with the permission of the manager, in the hotel car park at the top of the hill. Suitable payment was exchanged in the form of a batch of fresh cheese straws for the staff.

'How absolutely wonderful.' Josh emerged from the back studio to greet his daughter. His once-vibrant red hair, now turned snow white, brushed the ceiling beams, forcing him to stoop as he kissed her.

The two up, two down cottage was so small there was barely room for her parents to move around in it. When Tamara came to visit, if the weather was fine they sat outside the front door to eat their meals. No-one minded. The moment their little table was erected, it was as if an invitation had been issued to any of their neighbours who were around.

Easels would be set up around the table and paint mixed alongside the salads and seafood. Vibrant conversation flowed from the artists who loved to talk and put the world to rights as they worked and ate.

'I'm only here for the weekend,' Tamara explained, hugging her father.

'A weekend with the two most beautiful women in the world is better than a lifetime with anyone else,' Josh boomed out.

Everything about her father was larger than life. His paintings were bold expressions of his art, unique and eagerly sought after by serious collectors. His work was a total contrast to that of his wife, Merrill. Her art was a humorous reflection of the absurdities of every day life.

Merrill adored ridiculous situations and her domestic scenes depicted her quirky sense of style. The little gallery in the centre of the village always displayed examples of Josh's and Merrill's work and both of them had a regular following.

'Let's go down to the beach,' Josh

suggested. 'I'll throw a picnic together and we'll spend the day lazing by the sea putting the world to rights.'

'We'll go to the cove.' Merrill linked arms with her daughter, noticing the lines of tiredness around her eyes.

Josh's idea of throwing a picnic together was often no more than a bottle of wine and a hunk of cheese.

'Once your father gets back in that studio of his, he'll probably forget all about the picnic anyway.'

After a brief detour via the baker's the two women strolled down the path towards the beach. Like their cottage, the cove was tucked away between the cliffs.

Tamara inhaled the smells of salt air and seaweed and sighed.

'Your back isn't paining you?' Merrill asked, frowning as her daughter stumbled on a cobblestone.

'I'm just a bit stiff after the long drive,' Tamara admitted.

'You should have come to us to convalesce,' her mother chided her.

'I wouldn't want to crowd you and Josh,' Tamara replied.

Ever since she had been a child, Tamara had called her parents by their first names. Her mother had only been nineteen years old when her daughter was born and at times she seemed more like a glamorous older sister than her mother. Despite the age difference between her father and Merrill, he was young for his years and when the three of them got together, it was as if they were old friends catching up on the gossip.

'You could never do that, my darling,' Merrill picked her way carefully over the rocks. 'Here, you'd better hold these,' she thrust a paper bag of pasties at her daughter. 'I don't want to drop them.'

With much laughter and false alarms, the two women finally reached their destination with all their baggage intact. Together they settled down on the sand.

Tamara closed her eyes for a few

moments. The drive down had been stressful and her back ached more than she had let on to her mother. After an early start, road works and traffic jams had held her up, together with the increased weekend traffic.

Merrill cast a sideways glance at her daughter. She let her snooze for a few moments before she asked, 'What's the real reason for your visit, my darling?'

Tamara slowly opened her eyes.

'Sorry, didn't mean to fall asleep on you.' She sipped some mineral water to clear her dry throat.

'Is it Adam Penrose?' Merrill asked.

Tamara gaped at her mother. 'I've always suspected you possessed supernatural powers,' she laughed, 'now I'm convinced of it.'

'You're not mooning over Myles Johnson?'

'No,' Tamara admitted. 'I don't think about him much at all these days.'

'Good, because he wasn't right for you, my darling. I didn't say anything because it's not my position to interfere.' Merrill stroked her daughter's arm. 'But I am glad you are over him. Adam Penrose is the man for you.'

'You forget what happened between us,' Tamara reminded her mother.

'Your timing was wrong, that's all. I'm glad he's walked back into your life.'

'How do you know?'

Merrill smiled. 'It's not rocket science or second sight. You live in Hayminster, five miles from Waterman's Wharf, so it is inevitable your paths should cross.'

'Put like that, I suppose it is.' Tamara paused. 'How did you know Adam has moved into Waterman's Wharf?'

'He sent me a change of address card,' Merrill replied simply.

'You kept in touch?'

'From time to time. So if it's not Adam or Myles, what is worrying you?'

Sitting on the beach beside her mother, Tamara began to suspect she had overreacted to all that had happened. When neither Phyllis nor

Adam had contacted her again during the week following Phyllis's car breakdown, Tamara knew she needed a change of scenery and where better to find it than a weekend in Cornwall? To hear her mother's down to earth common sense, and to laugh at her father's outrageous Celtic sense of humour was the best medicine in the world.

'You're right. I did bump into Adam again recently.'

'And?' Merrill prompted when Tamara lapsed into silence.

'His great-aunt Phyllis, well, to cut a long story short, a man came to collect her car. It had broken down on my forecourt.'

Merrill's generous mouth curved into a smile. 'You're being a little sketchy on detail, darling. I trust there's more?'

'He didn't look like any car mechanic I know. He sounded Eastern European and he wanted to speak to Phyllis but when I told him he couldn't, and that she wasn't at the barn, well, he didn't believe me.'

'Where was she?'

'That's another thing, you see, she's disappeared.'

'My goodness.' Merrill's deep blue eyes widened in surprise. 'You are leading an exciting life.'

'She used to live at Bailey's Barn. Adam told me.'

'Darling.' Merrill's brow cleared. 'Are you talking about Phyllis Morosotkova?'

'No, her name is Phyllis Morton.'

Merrill brushed aside Tamara's interruption.

'I met her once at a gallery viewing. She was staying down here. She was actually rather grand and scared me a bit, but I liked her. She suggested it was too boring to stay inside all day, and why didn't we go out for a drive along the coast after she'd freshened up?'

'And?'

'She went to powder her nose and never came back. It seems she went off with someone else. When she did eventually re-appear she said she had wanted to enjoy the autumn colours. Do you know I think she'd forgotten all about me?'

'That sounds like the Phyllis Morton I met.'

'There was a man in the background, another lofty type. He didn't look at all pleased when she introduced him to the young man she'd driven off with. All in all it was a very strange afternoon, even by artistic standards.' Merrill smiled prettily. 'So there you are, if we are talking about the same person I'm sure nothing's happened to her and there's no need to worry about it.'

'That's what Adam said. He said his aunt had a habit of doing that sort of thing before he accused me of wasting his time.'

Tamara was still fuming over the unjust accusation and would have said more if her mother hadn't asked in a careful voice, 'How is he?'

Tamara pondered whether or not to tell her mother about his injury. Instead, she contented herself with,

'He's writing a book and Phyllis is helping him.'

'I see. Well should you see him again, give him my love.'

Tamara scooped up some fine-grained sand and let it drift through her fingers. The seagulls circled overhead, ready to pounce on the remains of their picnic. The sun was now slanting towards the sea, casting an orange tinge on the horizon.

'We were right not to wait for your father,' Merrill offered Tamara the last of the pasties. 'We would have passed out with hunger. Eccentrics run in our family too. He's probably forgotten all about us.'

'Do you think we ought to get back before he starts bellowing for you?' Tamara asked with a guilty start. She hadn't realised so much time had passed. It was always the same when she got chatting with her mother.

'Let him bellow,' Merrill leaned back against a convenient rock, a mischievous gleam in her eyes. 'It'll do him good. I intend to make the most of the sun before it disappears into the sea.'

The sound of the waves lapping the shore reminded Tamara of her childhood, when she and her mother used to spend hours on the beach, scratching around for shells and seaweed, exploring the caves, having fun. The long holidays seemed to stretch out forever. Merrill would always stop work for the summer and devote her time to her daughter.

'These days will never return,' she would say, 'and too soon they will be gone. We must enjoy them while we can.'

'Have you heard from Myles?' Merrill asked.

Tamara shook her head. 'He and Jasmine move in different circles now, and I've moved on too. I had to leave a lot of things behind when I gave up modelling.'

'You are happy?'

'Very. I love living in Hayminster and I've had the barn redecorated. I wish you and Josh would visit.'

'You know your father behaves like a bear with a sore head if he's away from his beloved studio for more than a day.'

'You could come on your own.'

'And I don't like being separated from your father for more than a day either.' Merrill's eyes twinkled again. 'Aren't we a boring old couple?'

'I wish all marriages were as happy as yours.' Tamara glanced at her mother with affection.

'And the new business? Is it flourishing?'

'I've got several regular customers now. My cheese straws were voted best savoury snack by one of my ladies' groups.'

Merrill squeezed her daughter's fingers. 'It's good to hear you laugh again.'

'There wasn't much to laugh about when Myles was having his business problems.'

'And you really are over him?'

'Really and truly,' Tamara replied with a smile.

'That pleases me. Now we must get you together with Adam Penrose again.'

'No,' Tamara protested, already regretting having mentioned his name.

Before she could say any more there was a loud shout behind them. Merrill shaded her eyes against the sunshine and looked towards the rocks.

'I think your father's remembered where we are.' She made a face. 'He's looking hungry too. Did you eat the last pasty?'

'I think I did.' Tamara searched the bag in vain. 'There're only a few crumbs left.'

'I suppose you haven't got any of your cheese straws to hand?' Merrill enquired as a shadow behind them blotted out the sun.

'Sorry, I gave them all to the manager of the Sea View Hotel when I parked my car. Hello, Josh,' Tamara greeted her father. 'Did you remember the bread and cheese?'

'You were supposed to bring the

food,' he roared at them. Josh's bushy eyebrows met his shock of white hair in an expression of outrage.

'If I'd known where you'd gone I would have come looking for you earlier.'

'It was also your suggestion we came down to the cove.'

'No it wasn't. I wish you wouldn't go off without telling me,' he complained.

'Look at the pair of you,' Tamara teased them affectionately, 'squabbling like children.'

'That's because I'm hungry and my work hasn't gone well,' Josh lowered his voice to a grumble.

'Then let me cook you an early supper,' Tamara suggested, 'al fresco?'

'Bit late for the day's catch,' Josh kicked a stray shell with his sandaled foot.

'Then we'll eat out,' Merrill suggested.

'I'm not going to that fancy place on the front. The chef was most indignant when I told him his lobster sauce was too rich. He told me I don't know how to cook.'

'You don't, my darling,' Merrill pointed out, 'but that didn't stop you trying to tell him how to do a lobster thermidor, did it?'

'Fellow had the nerve to suggest we weren't welcome at his restaurant unless we kept our opinions to our ourselves.' Josh glared at Tamara.

'In that case,' she soothed down her father's ruffled feathers, 'why don't I conjure up one of my specials? You have got the ingredients for a fish stew somewhere in the cottage, Merrill?'

'I have indeed, and you do have the most wonderful ideas, darling. That's exactly what we need, a fresh fish stew, simmering in one of your lovely sauces. Now come along.'

A Possible Intruder

By the time Tamara drew into the courtyard of Bailey's Barn, the light was already fading from the day. She had left it as late as possible before starting the long drive home. Merrill had wanted her daughter to stay over for another night.

'I must get back,' Tamara insisted, 'I've several jobs on my books and I like to be on hand for my customers in case anything should go wrong.'

'Well, don't leave it so long before you visit us next time,' Josh insisted as he watch her load her car with all the bits and pieces Merrill had put out for her.

'Just some fruit cake,' Merrill explained. 'Josh eats far too much of it, and he's putting on weight, whereas you, my darling, are as slender as a reed.'

'You don't have to,' Tamara tried to protest.

'That's what mothers are for,' Merrill held up a packet. 'One or two pretty scarves I bought from the local craft shop and what else is there? Oh yes, two fresh lobster in the cold bag. Be sure to put them in the fridge the moment you get home,' she instructed Tamara, squashing another supermarket carrier into the only spare space she could in the car.

'You spoil me,' Tamara tried to protest.

'Of course I do, you're my daughter, my only child.'

The next moment Tamara was enveloped in one of her father's bear hugs.

'Ring the moment you arrive, you know your mother won't settle until you do.' His voice was gruff in her ear.

'I will, I promise.' Tamara hugged him back. 'Now I really do have to go if I want to get home today.'

★   ★   ★

Tamara climbed out of the driving seat and stretched her aching limbs. The barn was in darkness and for a moment she wished there was someone to open the door for her and welcome her into a warm family home.

A light breeze ruffled the trees and Tamara thrust on her jumper. The nights were still chilly and Hayminster didn't have the benefit of the milder Cornish climate.

Tamara caught a movement from behind the trees out of the corner of her eye.

'Hello?' she called out. 'Is anybody there?'

She walked slowly towards the copse. Was her tired eyesight playing a trick on her after the long drive?

She waited for a few moments, but whatever it was, it had gone. Suspecting it had probably been a rabbit in the undergrowth or a bird, she turned back to the car and began unloading her luggage.

An hour or so later she settled down

to a scratch supper of baked beans on toast, with a Mozart symphony on in the background. The barn creaked comfortably around her. The low lighting she had chosen to complement her warm colour scheme cast gentle shadows on the walls of the living room, a gentle contrast to the brilliant colours of Cornwall.

Remembering her promise, Tamara picked up her mobile phone and rang her. parents to announce her safe arrival home.

'I am so pleased to hear that, darling.' It was Merrill who replied, raising her voice against a bellow in the background. 'I can't talk now. Your father is having a crisis, something to do with his paint mix, you understand? Sleep well.'

Tamara replaced the receiver with a smile. Where Josh was concerned there was always a crisis over something. She finished her supper and after washing up her plate, decided to water the plants on the terrace before indulging in a warm aromatic bath and having an early night.

An owl hooted from the copse. The light from the waxing crescent of the new moon cast ghostly shadows on the terrace. Tamara shivered, aware not for the first time of the remoteness of Bailey's Barn.

Tamara filled her watering can then frowned. Her hydrangea plants had been moved and she was sure she had swept the terrace before she left, but now it was a mess of leaves and clods of earth. She would have suspected an animal was responsible for the debris only there was no way a squirrel or a fox could have actually moved the plant container. It was horse-trough shaped, and heavy.

The flagstones were wet from what Tamara suspected had been an earlier shower. In the darkness it was difficult to make out whether the damp patches were human footprints or evidence of intrusion by local wildlife.

Tamara shivered. She was not a

naturally nervous person, but she couldn't shake off the feeling that someone had been snooping around, but who? There were no other signs of an attempted break in and apart from the moved pot plants everything else looked as usual.

She swept up the mess, straightened the plant holder, then closed the back door, careful to double lock it and pulled the blind down. If the press were still intent on invading her privacy it would be wise to take every precaution. Pouring herself a glass of wine, she made her way upstairs. After a soak in the bath and sipping her drink, she fell asleep the moment her head touched the pillow.

The next morning sun streamed through the kitchen window. Tamara opened the windows wide letting in the warm spring air. Her fears of the night before subsided.

The contract gardeners had arrived and were busy mowing the lawn and cutting back the overgrown greenery.

Their cheerful whistling and sounds of activity convinced Tamara her suspicions had been nothing more than the result of an over-tired and over-active imagination, something which was the result of having been the attention of intrusive media focus. Her story had long since faded from the headlines.

The front doorbell rang. Stifling a sigh over the unexpected interruption, she went through to the hallway to answer it.

'Phyllis.' She stepped back in surprise at the sight of the woman standing on her doorstep.

'Hello, dear.' The older woman greeted her with a kiss. 'Am I forgiven?' She thrust a bunch of early summer flowers at her. 'Peace offering.'

'Where have you been?' Tamara demanded, doing her best to look stern. It wasn't easy with Phyllis smiling at her in such a friendly fashion and looking suitably contrite.

'It's a long story better told over a

cup of your delicious coffee?'

'As long as you promise to stay on the premises while we drink it,' Tamara insisted, 'and tell me exactly what happened.'

'Of course, darling. Scouts' honour,' a chastened Phyllis promised as she followed Tamara into the kitchen. 'If you've got any of your lovely nibbles on the go as well, they'd be most welcome. By the way, where have you been?' she asked. 'I called round yesterday and peered in all the windows, but there was no one here.'

'I've been to visit my parents,' Tamara replied, relieved to realise that the disturbance on the patio was Phyllis's doing.

'Down in Cornwall?'

'Yes. How did you know?'

'Adam told me the painter, Merrill Cardroc, is your mother.'

'Yes, she is.'

'Then the divine Josh Cameron must be your father.'

Tamara placed a plate of fresh scones

on the table and Phyllis attacked one with gusto.

'I really do enjoy coming to you for coffee,' she said through a mouthful of raspberry jam. 'You are the best baker in the world. If ever you want a reference let me know.'

'Thank you. I suppose you missed breakfast again?'

'I never seem to get round to it, there's always so much else to do. You know, I tried to bake a cake once. It sank in the middle and we used it as a doorstop. It lasted all year until someone threw it out because it was growing whiskers and becoming a bit of a health hazard.'

It was impossible to feel annoyed with Phyllis for long. She was so candid about her failings, and so ready to praise other's strengths.

'My mother said you've met her.'

'Have I?' Phyllis spread more jam on the second half of her scone. 'When was that?'

'At an art viewing.'

Phyllis pulled a face. 'I generally avoid those affairs like the plague. They are always so stuffy and how are you supposed to juggle a drink with a sausage on a stick and make polite conversation to boring dignitaries, full of their own self importance?'

'Not all viewings are like that,' Tamara protested.

'They are in my experience.' Phyllis paused from spreading butter over another scone. 'Merrill Cardroc, yes, how silly of me, of course I remember her. She was the only breath of fresh air at that dreadful society do. Some big noise was opening up a new gallery or something. The place was more than usually full of pompous people, trying to pretend they knew about art.' Phyllis's eyes twinkled at the memory. 'I escaped with a young man half my age.'

'After you promised to go for a drive with my mother.'

'Did I?' Phyllis dropped her laden scone back onto the plate. 'Whatever must she think of me? Please apologise to her on my behalf. I don't do that sort of thing on purpose, you know.'

'It's all right. You're lucky my mother doesn't easily take offence. After years of marriage to my father, she understands the artistic temperament.'

'Actually,' Phyllis's eyes narrowed, 'now I look at you, I can see from where you inherit your model looks. You're very much like your mother and you've got your father's blue eyes.'

Aware they were in danger of straying off course, Tamara steered the conversation firmly back to the matter of Phyllis's disappearance.

'So what happened after your car broke down?' she demanded. 'You owe me an explanation.'

'I know, darling. I am so sorry.'

'Adam was very annoyed to arrive and find you weren't here,' Tamara added.

'He always is. Honestly, how my sister could have produced such a grumpy grandson I will never know. He went on alarmingly about it afterwards.

He could lecture for the county.'

'You'll get another lecture from me, too, if you don't tell me what happened,' Tamara said, annoyed that neither Phyllis nor Adam had seen fit to update her on the situation. 'Adam more or less accused me of wasting his time.'

'I told you men talk nothing but nonsense.' Phyllis gave a self-justified nod of her head. 'The truth is I went out into the garden to look around.' Phyllis glanced out of the window. 'By the way, who are those divine young men clipping your hedge?'

'Don't change the subject,' Tamara insisted.

Phyllis blinked then recognising the steely resolve in Tamara's voice continued with a sigh.

'You were ages on the phone to Adam. I didn't realise you used to be an item. It must have been when I was away on one of my African treks?' Tamara refused to take the bait and forced to carry on in the face of her silence Phyllis said, 'Anyway, after I'd finished looking around the garden, it was so nice in the fresh air I sort of kept strolling. Then I realised I was halfway down the lane and it was just as far to walk back as to go on, so I went on.'

'All the way to Waterman's Wharf? That's over five miles.'

'I'm fitter than I look, but actually when I got up to the main road an old friend was driving by. He recognised me and stopped his car. We went off and had some lunch together.'

'Phyllis, that was ten days ago.'

'That long?' Phyllis raised her eyebrows. 'I hope you weren't worried sick about me. When I got back to Adam's apartment, there was a message for me from my neighbour. One of my pipes had burst and water was gushing everywhere. I had to go home immediately. It was very naughty of Adam not to update you.' She cast Tamara what could have been interpreted as a sly look, 'but he has been very busy with Suzie Fairbrother.'

Again Tamara refused to rise to Phyllis's bait.

'And your car?'

'What about it?'

'Have you heard anything?'

'Er, no.' Phyllis looked suitably vague.

'The man who came to collect it was most disappointed to discover you didn't live here any more.'

'Is that so?' Phyllis's smile was a shade weaker than normal.

'In fact, I had quite a job convincing him you weren't here. I don't think he believed me, either.'

'I did move out in rather a rush,' Phyllis admitted, 'and I didn't get round to telling everyone. I do hope you're not bothered by any more of my friends.' She slid a card across the table. 'You can always tell them to contact me on this number.'

'Is this the number of your mobile phone that you keep forgetting to top up?' Tamara queried.

'I do get the messages, eventually,'

Phyllis evaded a direct reply. Tamara was beginning to recognise her style. If she didn't like the question, she didn't answer it. 'Now you must be busy. I'd better not outstay my welcome.'

'How did you get here today?'

'Adam's hired a car. I hate driving the thing. Vladimir never complained if I crashed the gears, but this one is an automatic and I'm never sure what gear I'm in. It's all most confusing. Reverse is very strange and I'm terrified I'm going to back into something important.'

'Are you still helping Adam with his work?' Tamara asked as Phyllis finally lapsed into silence.

'That's another thing, he keeps going on at me to sort out my photos and notes, but who wants to live in the past? This wretched book is proving a millstone around my neck.' Without warning Phyllis leaned forward and tucked a stray lock of hair behind Tamara's ear. 'I do wish you and Adam would get together again. I mean, I like

Suzie, but she never stops talking. If you did get back together with Adam he probably wouldn't be half so bad tempered and I would be free to pursue my own pursuits.'

A tap on the window from one of the workmen created a welcome diversion and saved Tamara the necessity of replying.

'I'll see myself out.' Phyllis blew her another kiss.

As Tamara made more coffee for the workmen there was the sound of a car being started up on the forecourt. Tamara held her breath, hoping Phyllis had managed to find the right gear and wasn't about to reverse into the contractor's van.

It was mid-afternoon before Tamara had a chance to check her telephone messages. There were two. She flicked the switch for the first one.

'Tammy? Adam here. Sorry I didn't get back to you sooner, I've been a bit busy. Just to let you know Phyllis is safe and sound. I've told her to come and apologise to you personally when she's sorted out the drama with her burst pipes.' There was a murmur of another voice in the background. Tamara wondered if it was Suzie's as she listened to the end of Adam's message. 'By the way, if you do have a rethink, my job offer still holds. That's all. Hope you're well.'

The message clicked off.

Not giving herself time to think about Adam's relationship with Suzie, Tamara pressed the button for the second message.

'Tamara?' She stiffened at the sound the voice she would have recognised anywhere. It was a voice that for the last six months she had been doing her best to forget. 'It's Myles. How are you? I need to talk to you. It's rather urgent. Can you ring this number as soon as possible?'

An Uncomfortable Reunion

The carriage drive leading down to the house was long and leafy. Tamara began to wonder if she was ever going to reach the end. It seemed ages since she had passed through the wrought-iron gates indicating that she had arrived at her destination. Her stomach churned at the thought of meeting up with Myles again. His offer of some catering work was not one she cherished and she had tried to turn it down.

'It's got to be you,' Myles insisted down the telephone when she initially tried to protest. 'You're almost family.'

The fee he mentioned made her eyes water and overcoming her scruples regarding the delicacy such an assignment would entail, Tamara agreed to meet up with him and Jasmine Fenwick to discuss the finer details of the finger buffet they were planning.

Just as she was wondering what Jasmine Fenwick really thought about the situation — having your partner's ex around hardly made for a peaceful scenario — the trees cleared and a Queen Anne house came into view.

Tamara's breath caught in her throat. No wonder Myles had been impressed. Without knowing any of its history she could see the property had been beautifully tended over the years and not fallen prey to tasteless extensions or modernisation. It followed the clean classical architectural lines of the period and stayed true to its provenance.

Tamara took a few moments out to enjoy its style as it basked in the afternoon sunshine. The grounds were also well maintained and very different from those surrounding Bailey's Barn. Her garden was an organic riot of plants and wild flowers. Here the lawns were manicured to within an inch of their lives and the hedges trimmed to perfection. A rueful smile curved Tamara's lips. For all its well-tended beauty, she would far rather be sitting in one of her wonky deckchairs in her own slightly chaotic back garden, sipping her favourite camomile tea while nature was allowed to do its own thing around her.

Climbing back in her car, Tamara continued on down the drive. As she drove onto the forecourt, the front door opened and three Labrador dogs bounded out.

'Heel,' a female voice shouted imperiously. 'Barney, back. Quiet!' she now bellowed as their barking reached new levels. 'Saunders, take them, please.' She gave a crisp order to a man standing behind her.

He reached out a hand and dragged the exuberant dogs back inside.

'Sorry,' Jasmine called over to Tamara. 'You can get out now, the coast's clear.'

The two girls had only met once before, at a summer garden party, on the occasion of their host's eightieth birthday. A huge marquee had been erected on the lawn of a country house. Champagne had flowed and Tamara and the other models, wearing especially commissioned day dresses, had mingled with the partygoers. It had been the day Myles and Jasmine had met for the first time too. At the time Tamara had not noticed their attraction to each other.

She had been busy networking on the orders of her agency. The models were there as ambassadors for their agency. It was their remit to show off their dresses to best effect, in the hope of obtaining new orders for the clothes they were wearing. Each girl had been allowed to take a partner and Myles had been more than pleased to join Tamara for the event, as her guest.

The daughter of the owner of the house had invited Jasmine Fenwick. To Tamara's trained eye she had looked elegant in her fetchingly simple turquoise shift dress with matching bolero jacket. The outfit provided a contrast to her stunning red hair and she saw more than one male cast appreciative glances in her direction. It was only later that Tamara discovered Jasmine was the daughter of a high profile businessman, a self-made man who dealt in engineering components. According to Myles business was booming.

'Lovely to see you again,' Jasmine gushed at her, then kissed Tamara on both cheeks.

She was wearing a French perfume that Tamara recognised. It was one she had never liked, its fragrance being too overpowering for her taste and in her opinion inappropriate for an English country garden.

'It's good to see you too,' Tamara reciprocated.

'It was so kind of you to drop everything for us. I was doubtful about approaching you, but Myles insisted you would want to help. I presume you've got masses of samples of your work to show us?'

'My books are in the car and I've got letters of recommendation.' The ladies' circle had been more than generous in their praise and given Tamara free rein to use their endorsements of her services.

'Bring them through. Daddy's out the back with Myles. He is so looking forward to getting together with you again. He was only saying the other day how much he misses you.'

It was all Tamara could do not to raise her eyebrows. Remembering the brutal details of their split, she wondered if perhaps Myles's conscience was tweaking him or maybe Jasmine was being economical with the truth.

The back garden was laid out in a similar design to the front. A rose pergola acted as a natural barrier half way down the lawn, beyond which Tamara could see a high wall enclosing a kitchen garden.

A red faced man stood up to greet Tamara as she emerged onto the terrace.

'Bob Fenwick,' he introduced himself, not remembering they had already met. His handshake was firm and threatened to crush Tamara's fingers, 'and of course you know Myles, don't you?'

The older man's shrewd brown eyes surveyed Tamara waiting for her reaction.

'Hi there.' Myles's attempt at laid back casual fell awkwardly flat, as did his attempt to embrace Tamara.

She stepped back and contented herself with squeezing his arm. No way was she kissing Myles with his new fiancée and her father looking on. She hadn't known what to expect from this first meeting. Strangely it hardly made any impression on her at all unlike the impact of her reunion with Adam Penrose.

Tamara noticed Myles's figure was showing the effects of too much good living. The designer polo shirt he was wearing was a little tight across his chest revealing the suggestion of a spare tyre around his midriff and although it was early in the afternoon, he had already opened a bottle of wine.

'Would you like a glass?' he held up a bottle of French white.

Tamara shook her head.

'Perhaps Miss Cameron would prefer something more refreshing?' Jasmine's father suggested. 'A fruit juice?'

'That would be lovely. Thank you,' Tamara accepted a cool glass of lemonade and lime from Mr Fenwick. 'Please,' she smiled at him, 'call me Tamara.'

'Then I must insist you call me Bob.' He held out a chair for her.

'Myles,' Jasmine's voice broke into the atmosphere. 'I'd like a glass of fruit juice too please.'

'Certainly, of course.' He obeyed her command with alacrity, then spent more moments ensuring her chair was correctly placed in the shade in order to shield her complexion from the sun. Scurrying around to obey Jasmine's every command, Myles reminded

Tamara of an overeager lap dog.

'So, what have you got to show us?' he asked when everyone eventually settled down.

'Before we discuss any business,' Bob Fenwick raised a hand, 'I hope you won't take my request the wrong way, Miss, er, Tamara.' He opened a buff folder, 'but I would like you to sign a confidentiality clause.'

Tamara blinked, not sure she had heard him correctly. 'Isn't that a little over the top for a finger buffet?' she asked.

'I'm sure Tamara can be trusted to be discreet,' Myles butted in.

'Nevertheless,' it was Jasmine who now spoke, 'I think Daddy and I would be happier if she signed the contract. That way if anything should leak out, we shall know exactly who is responsible.' Jasmine turned a brittle smile in Tamara's direction. 'It's nothing personal, I'm sure you understand, Tamara, only a person in my position has to be careful.'

'All my client details are confidential, unless they're paid for by the public purse,' Tamara replied.

She glanced down at the legally drawn up document Bob had placed in front of her.

'For the record?' he held up a pen.

Tamara read it through carefully. In her time she had seen many such documents and understood what they were all about, but this was the first one she had been asked to sign in her current line of business.

'May I ask a question?'

'Go right ahead,' Bob replied.

'As I understand it, you are throwing a small reception for twenty people in your garden?'

'Correct.'

'That is within your capabilities?' Jasmine enquired, again with an edge to her voice.

Tamara ignored the question. 'Why is such a document needed for a low key affair?'

There was a short pause before

Myles admitted, 'Because it will be Jasmine's and my wedding reception.'

Tamara took a few moments out to absorb his words.

'You're getting married?'

'Yes,' Myles replied, not looking her in the eye.

'Congratulations.'

'And we don't want news of it to be leaked to the press beforehand,' Jasmine snapped.

'Surely, in the circumstances wouldn't a more upmarket caterer be a suitable choice for your requirements?'

'My daughter thought a small reception in the garden for family and a few close friends would be better than a large affair attracting media attention. We don't want references to Myles's past spoiling the happy day.'

'People have short memories.' Tamara didn't want to defend Myles, but a small part of her resented the slur on his character. Myles had his faults, but he had tried to do his best to salvage the failing business.

He cast Tamara a look of gratitude.

'And surely no-one is still interested in the story? It's old history now.'

'Maybe,' Bob conceded, 'but I still feel a small affair is called for.'

Tamara wondered why neither Jasmine nor Myles were expressing their preferences, it was their wedding reception, low key or not.

'I am currently engaged in confidential high profile negotiations regarding a takeover,' Bob Fenwick explained, 'and everything I do is also subject to scrutiny. If the press get hold of my daughter's wedding details the story will be plastered all over the financial pages.'

'Wouldn't you prefer a grander affair?' Tamara asked Jasmine, 'or you could get married abroad? That's a very popular choice these days.'

'We'll hold a ball later in the year after Daddy's business thing is completed,' Jasmine replied.

'I can assure you, Tamara,' Bob insisted, 'there are no hidden provisos in the contract. It's a straightforward document stating that you will not reveal any of the details of my daughter's impending marriage to Myles Johnson. Once you've signed it, you are guaranteeing that anything you do overhear will go no further.'

'I'm not sure I'm the right person for the job,' Tamara prevaricated, still uneasy about the commission. 'There are many established companies who are better suited for this sort of thing.'

'We thought given your previous association with Myles,' Bob paused, 'that you could be trusted not to reveal any of the details. You also have a vested interest in wanting to stay out of the public eye.'

'I'm flattered, of course,' Tamara played for time. The job would be a boost to her earnings, but was it worth the risk? Jasmine struck her as a possible demanding client.

'We are offering you a generous fee.'

'Are the guests being asked to sign similar disclaimers?' Tamara asked.

Jasmine's response was a haughty 'I think the family can be trusted to keep quiet about the ceremony.'

'Will your ex-wife be attending?' she asked Bob Fenwick.

'Of course my mother will be here. Every girl wants her mother with her on her wedding day,' Jasmine snapped.

'And what about her partner?'

Tamara could see Bob Fenwick was irked by her questions.

'Her new husband will be attending, of course, if his schedule permits.'

It was another story that had briefly made the headlines. Jasmine's mother, who before her marriage to Bob Fenwick had been a minor television actress, had recently re-married a rising celebrity whose name was already being put forward for various awards.

'They are constantly flying over from America. There won't be a problem,' Jasmine insisted. 'Everyone will assume they are here for another business visit.'

'I could perhaps see my way to increasing your fee if you feel the work involved will create extra demands on your time?' Bob offered.

'When exactly will the wedding be?' Tamara asked. 'Summer is my busiest season. I may already be booked.'

'I had hoped you would sign the contract before we revealed the details,' Bob said.

'We will be getting married the middle weekend of July, on the Saturday,' Jasmine said.

Tamara opened her diary. The day was blank due to a recent cancellation.

'Very well,' she nodded, making a note on the open page.

'I knew Daddy could talk you round with the offer of an increased fee,' Jasmine crowed, 'he always says everyone has their price.'

Biting her lip, Tamara ignored her as she signed the two copies of the contract, keeping one for herself. She still wasn't sure if she had done the right thing, but Bob Fenwick was an astute businessman and she was sure his word was his bond.

'Now,' Jasmine gushed, 'we shall need to cater for all sorts of special diets. Mummy doesn't touch carbs and her partner only eats fruit at the weekend. I can't touch egg whites and I'm vegetarian. Daddy needs to watch his weight so fruitcake is out. Everything has to be certified organic. I'm not going too fast for you?'

There was a flicker of a sympathetic smile from Myles as Tamara did her best to keep up with Jasmine's requests.

'I'll manage,' she murmured, more than glad that her model training had prepared her for this sort of thing.

She would need to recruit some temporary help. Already the generous advance Bob Fenwick had promised was looking seriously inadequate. Special requests didn't come cheap and Jasmine sounded as though she had only just started on her list.

A Pepperoni Pizza

Still pondering on the strange events of the day, Tamara stopped in Hayminster on the way home. She needed to do some food shopping. The provisions her mother had given her had finally run out.

Parking her car in the centre she grabbed her bag and headed towards the local greengrocer. She'd seen displays of early strawberries and new potatoes outside and she needed to top up on her salad supplies. Ambling down the main street, she took time out to enjoy the sight of the wooden weatherboarded cottages surrounded by white picket fences. The romance of this part of Kent had been one of the reasons why she had moved back to the area.

Years ago the Hawkhurst Gang had terrorised the area, with their nightly forays inspiring the famous poem by

Rudyard Kipling, but these days a gentler way of life prevailed. Now the county was better known for its hop gardens and oast houses and the blossom route was a popular tourist attraction.

The afternoon sun was warm on Tamara's back and she was glad she had worn a summer blouse and a peasant-style flowing skirt for her meeting with Myles and Jasmine. A part of her couldn't help feeling sorry for Myles. Jasmine and her father made a formidable pair and she was sure Myles would have his work cut out satisfying his fiancée's every whim. For all her delicate femininity Jasmine was a tough cookie.

Although she had expressed a preference for a budget style reception, Tamara didn't doubt she too would have her hands full dealing with her client's every whim. Tamara hoped that after her career in the modelling business there wasn't much she didn't know about artistic temperament and that she was up to the task.

'Can I tempt you to some of our best early English potatoes?' the greengrocer greeted Tamara with a smile. 'Go down a treat with fresh summer salad.'

Victim to the greengrocer's sales patter Tamara's shopping bag was soon bulging. 'Think I've bought too much,' she made a face. Her back muscles reminded her with an angry twinge not to overdo things as she tried to lift it.

'Need some help?'

She stepped back and looked into Adam's smiling face.

'You're not wearing your sling.' She straightened up, instantly noting his free arm.

'The doctor says I can leave it off.' He flexed his shoulder muscles. 'Hardly notice my injury these days.' He picked up her bag with practised ease. 'So where are we going?'

Tamara was tempted to say she didn't need his help, but Adam was already walking off with her bag.

'Back to my car.'

'Have you had any lunch?' he asked as they strode along the pavement.

'It's half-past three.' Tamara glanced up at the church clock as they passed the fifteenth century church tower. 'Isn't it rather late for lunch?'

'Well I missed out. There was an unexpected emergency at the doctor's and I was delayed in the surgery.'

'Actually,' Tamara admitted, remembering the small dishes of nuts Jasmine had put out for them, 'I only had a few nibbles too.'

She unlocked the boot of her car and Adam deposited her bag.

'Fancy a pizza?' He nodded towards the Italian restaurant, 'by way of apology?'

'Sorry?'

'I was unbelievably rude to you the other day. I can only say my shoulder was hurting but I shouldn't have taken it out on you. I meant to say Phyllis was wasting my time, not you, but it came out all wrong. Next thing I knew we were having words. Friends?' he asked with a raised eyebrow.

'Friends.' Tamara smiled back at him. She had never been one to hold a grudge and she was feeling hungry. 'Will we get a pizza this time of day?'

'Giancarlo's a friend. We can but ask. Come on.'

'But of course,' Ginacarlo greeted them with smiles and handshakes. 'For you, Adam, I am always open and when you arrive escorted by a beautiful lady what Italian would say no? I will personally see to your order.'

They sat outside under one of the striped umbrellas, sipping some mint tea. The afternoon sun caught the natural chestnut highlights in Adam's hair. Today it didn't look quite so spiky and he was freshly shaven.

He ran a hand over his chin following the train of her thoughts.

'It's a bit easier to use a razor now. I only used to shave every other day because I looked pretty gruesome when I kept cutting myself.' A dimple deepened in his cheek. 'And I can now brush my hair properly too.'

'I wasn't . . . Tamara began to protest. He'd always been able to tune in on her wavelength.

'It's all right,' Adam held up a hand, 'I know I looked a bit like a scrubbing brush that had suffered a shock, but you should have seen the rest of me.'

Tamara flushed a deep shade of red.

'I meant,' Adam's eyes twinkled, 'that I was covered in bruises.'

'How's the book going?' Tamara asked in an attempt to move the conversation onto less personal matters.

'Slowly. I had no idea it would be such hard work. Give me a journalistic assignment any day.'

'What about Suzie?'

'Suzie from downstairs?'

'Isn't she helping you?'

'She's my neighbour's daughter. She was home on a short break, but she's gone back to uni. She did a bit of typing for me to earn some pocket money, that's all.'

108

'Phyllis said you spent a lot of time together.'

'There was nothing of a personal nature between us.'

'When I saw her she was kissing you rather enthusiastically,' Tamara said, then wished she hadn't, as a smile stretched across Adam's face.

'I thought that shadow at the window was you spying on us. She'd just heard she'd got straight *As* in her exams and being a naturally exuberant girl, she felt like kissing someone. I was only congratulating her. Do you have a problem with that?'

Tamara was pleased when Giancarlo created an interruption by delivering two piping hot pepperonis to their table.

'Here we are. Buon appetito.'

After he had produced a pepper mill and topped up their mint tea he left them alone again.

'I understand Phyllis has apologised to you?' Adam cut into his pizza.

'Yes.' The tang of crisp peppers and

herby cheese reminded Tamara how long it had been since breakfast and following Adam's example she cut into the cheesy crust of her pepperoni.

'The family are used to Phyllis's eccentricities, but I'm sorry she worried you. I'll make sure she doesn't do it again. I've given her the lecture.'

'She mentioned it,' Tamara said with a smile, 'and I won't worry now I know it's a family trait.'

'Apart from anything else,' Adam's easy-going face was set in an unaccustomed frown, 'it's a nuisance going round apologising for her behaviour. Not everyone is as understanding as you. I've had some very uncomfortable interviews in my time as I've tried to explain.'

Tamara finished her pizza and sat back with a satisfied sigh.

'Could you manage some zabaglione?' Adam asked.

'I shouldn't really,' Tamara protested.

Giancarlo caught the end of their conversation as he cleared away their plates. 'I do the best zabaglione outside of Tuscany.'

Tamara's token resistance crumbled.

'In that case, how can I refuse?' she laughed.

Beaming with pleasure Giancarlo bustled back to the kitchen.

'All my waistbands are getting tight,' Tamara protested. 'When I was modelling, creamy desserts were off the menu, so were pizza lunches. We were lucky if we were allowed a salad and if we were on a shoot we barely had time to eat even that.'

'Do you miss the life?' Adam asked.

Tamara shook her head. 'I was constantly living out of a suitcase and the erratic sleep patterns and time zones played havoc with my skin. I barely knew which country I was in. These days, I hardly bother with make-up and I can't remember the last time I visited the hairdresser.' She ran a finger through her ash blonde locks. 'Do I look like a scarecrow?'

The expression in Adam's eyes was

unreadable as he replied in a quiet voice, 'Not at all.'

'Now I love taking time out to watch the world go by,' Tamara said quickly, anxious to defuse any hidden subtext between them, as a trio of ducks padded through the grass opposite and splashed onto the pond.

A mother and little boy threw some stale bread after them and the ensuing undignified scenes as the ducks squabbled for the crumbs drew a smile to Tamara's lips.

'People say this part of the world is quiet, but over the past few weeks I think I've seen more activity here than in many of the capital cities I've visited.'

Adam raised an eyebrow. 'Tell me more,' he urged.

'There was Phyllis for a start,' Tamara began.

'True,' Adam agreed, 'you don't see her like in many countries.'

'Then there was the man who came to collect her car.'

The frown was back on Adam's

forehead. 'What about him?' he asked.

'Do you know him?'

'I'm not sure. Did he give you his name?'

Tamara shook her head. 'I think he was Eastern European. Anyway, he said he wanted to speak to Phyllis. I had difficulty convincing him she didn't live at Bailey's Barn any more.'

'What did he look like?'

'He was in his forties, pale skinned, slim and spoke with a strong accent.'

'The description would fit many of Phyllis's acquaintances. She runs an open house policy I can't keep up with her. She was probably a bit lax about telling people her new address.'

'That must be it,' Tamara agreed, 'and then it was Phyllis who was peering through my windows the other night so I needn't have worried about my plants being moved.'

'What?' Adam snapped back at her.

Tamara caught her breath, annoyed that she had let that bit of information slip.

'It was nothing really,' she insisted. 'When I got back from visiting my parents there were signs of a disturbance on the patio, footprints and a few leaves.'

'And you thought what?' Adam's journalistic skills kicked in.

'Nothing really. I only wondered if someone had been poking around and why. After that business with Myles,' she hesitated, 'well, the press were a bit of a nuisance. I was door-stepped for a while and some reporters are more persistent than others. They won't take 'no comment', for an answer, so I suppose it's made me hypersensitive. Earlier I thought I'd seen someone lurking around the bushes as I got out the car. Silly really. It was probably only an animal in the undergrowth and I mean who's interested in me now? I'm old news.'

'I apologise on behalf of the members of my profession,' Adam looked serious, 'some of them can be less than ethical in their attempts to get a story. We're not all like that,' he added.

'I know,' Tamara smiled, 'and thanks

for the apology.'

'Have you contacted the police?'

'What for?' Tamara protested. 'There was no damage and I don't actually know if there was anyone hanging around.'

'Promise you'll let me know if anything else happens?'

Tamara blinked. 'What sort of anything else?'

'If you think something's not right, let me know. Bailey's Barn is very remote.'

'Now you are scaring me.' Tamara half laughed, before she realised the expression in Adam's eyes told her he was serious.

'I don't like the idea of people poking around outside your property.'

'Adam, I promise you, you've no need to worry. I've got state of the art security and I'm pretty good at looking after myself.'

'You always were independent weren't you?' The corner of Adam's mouth softened as he looked at her.

'I've had to be,' Tamara answered simply. 'When you're on the catwalk you learn to fight your quarter.'

'I'm sure you do,' Adam agreed, 'but if you want the help of a war-torn hack with a dodgy shoulder, my offer still stands. We can't have reporters falling out of your trees in an attempt to get a story.'

'I'll remember that,' Tamara touched his hand in a gesture of thanks. His skin was warm and slightly rough.

For a brief moment they searched each other's eyes before Tamara removed her hand from Adam's. She hoped he hadn't felt her fingertips begin to tremble against his.

'So Phyllis tells me you've been down to Cornwall?' Adam appeared not to notice anything different about her as he changed the subject. 'Was it for any particular reason?'

'Only that it had been a while since I visited my parents.'

'How are they?'

'Josh was as irascible as ever.'

The fish stew supper had turned into a mini street party with Josh insisting the get together had been his idea. Only a sharp look from his wife stopped him from also taking the credit for cooking the fish stew as well.

'And your mother?' Adam asked.

'She was asking about you,' Tamara admitted with a reluctant smile. 'I think you made a hit there.'

'It's easy to like someone when you get along with them and they live in a lovely part of the world. Do you remember that bank holiday weekend?'

'The one that turned into a week?'

Josh, who also took a shine to Adam, insisted he be introduced to everyone in their circle of friends. Night after night there had been unexpected parties that had often gone on into the small hours. In the end Tamara had been pleased to return to work for some rest.

'Perhaps we'll all meet up again one day,' Adam said.

'Yes, perhaps.' Tamara glanced at her watch. 'I really should be getting back. How much do I owe you?'

'My treat,' Adam grabbed the bill

before Tamara had a chance to look at it.

'Are you sure?'

'If your conscience is troubling you, you can pay next time.'

Adam extracted his wallet from the pocket of his trousers.

'Thank you,' Tamara said in what she hoped was an impersonal voice. She was still uncertain about the situation with Adam and she was reluctant to go over old ground. She had let him down badly once and she didn't want to hurt him again.

'Talking of finances,' Adam said, busy counting out his change. 'Do you still keep in touch with Myles?'

Tamara hoped he did not detect the note of hesitation in her voice.

'He actually left a message on my answer phone while I was down in Cornwall,' she replied.

'What about?' Adam signalled to a hovering waiter.

'He wanted to meet up again. Actually that's where I've been this morning, catching up with him and Jasmine.'

Adam quirked an eyebrow, 'and is she as fragrant as her name implies?' he asked.

'She's certainly very beautiful,' Tamara admitted in reluctant acknowledgement.

'Her father owns a country house round here somewhere.'

'Yes. That's where we met up.'

'He's big in engineering, isn't he?'

'Yes.'

'Was he there too?'

'Yes, he was actually.' Tamara pretended a disinterest she was far from feeling. Adam was used to questioning people, and it wouldn't take him long to realise she was hiding something from him.

'When's the happy day?' Adam asked.

'Sorry?'

'The wedding? Didn't you say Myles and Jasmine are engaged?'

'Did I?' Tamara feigned more disinterest. This confidentiality clause was already proving to be a burden. 'To be honest, I had other things on my mind.'

'Of course,' Adam left a tip on the table for the waiter. 'Can you give me a lift back?' he asked with a smile. 'It would save me calling a taxi and it won't take you too much out of your way will it?'

'Not at all.' Tamara did her best to keep her voice casual.

They began walking towards Tamara's car. Adam slipped his hand into hers.

'If you've got time I could show you around Waterman's Wharf. Not the whole lot, just my little bit. It's got a fascinating history.'

Tamara extricated her fingers from Adam's in order to retrieve her keys from her handbag.

'Why not?' she smiled at him. 'I don't think I'm going to get much work done today anyway.'

She started the engine and reversing her car out of its parking space took the road towards Waterman's Wharf.

Renewing A Friendship

'Turn left here.' Adam directed Tamara to his personal parking space outside the entrance to number three, Waterman's Wharf. 'Phyllis has got the car today. I loaned it to her to do some shopping. Hope she doesn't wind up in Wales.' He grinned at Tamara. 'Come on, I'll show you round.'

Wishing she wasn't looking forward quite so much to seeing where Adam lived, and ignoring her conscience, which was telling her she should be working, Tamara followed Adam towards his front door.

'These warehouses were built in the middle of the nineteenth century,' Adam explained as he unlocked the door, 'and they are pretty solid. I've got the upper floor. Suzie's father lives below me. Like your father he's an artist and he says the early morning light is perfect for his work, especially at this time of year.'

Adam's working area was surprisingly tidy. His computer occupied one corner of a vast high-level room and another corner was piled high with books and files, some still stored in tea chests. There were a few pictures on the walls and an overstuffed sofa, covered in scarlet throws, was positioned against an upright wooden beam.

'I'll get round to sorting things out one day,' he said, as he crossed to the kitchen. 'Would you like some more tea if I can find any milk?' He opened the fridge door. There was nothing inside. 'Sorry, cancel that offer,' he apologised. 'It was Phyllis's turn to do the weekly supermarket sweep, looks like she forgot again.'

'You two are as bad as each other,' Tamara chided him, 'can't you organise a roster?'

'I've been injured,' Adam protested.

'You won't be able to play that card now you're not wearing your sling any more,' Tamara pointed out.

'It will be good to get back to some proper work,' Adam admitted, flexing his shoulder. 'Phyllis has been a help, but, well, she's not very practical. I dare not let her near the computer. She would wipe out all my files. She was supposed to be collating her own stuff, but I'm thinking of pulling the bit I was going to write about her. It's too much hassle and the publishers are getting a bit restless too. They keep asking for updates.'

'Poor old Phyllis,' Tamara sympathised.

'You've changed your tune,' Adam retaliated.

'I don't think she wanted to be in your book in the first place and that's her way of telling you.'

'Maybe you're right,' Adam agreed. 'Anyway, do you like my living area?' he asked with an eager smile. 'It's the first time I've had a place of my own that hasn't involved erecting a tent in the middle of nowhere, or been an iffy on-site mobile home with only very basic facilities.'

'You've done well,' Tamara congratulated him.

'Wooden beams support the main warehouse.' Adam slapped the flat of his hand against one. 'They give a warm feel to the place, don't you think?'

'Like I said, I'm impressed. How long have you been here?'

'I signed the contract about a year ago, but,' Adam indicated the tea chests, 'what with one thing and another, I've only spent about a month in actual residence, that's why I haven't properly unpacked yet. When I was first sent home I went up to Yorkshire to visit my parents and to do all the duty visits to my brothers and aunts.

'My mother was in seventh heaven nursing me. I let her have her way for a while, but when I started to regain the use of my arm,' Adam pulled a face, 'I escaped. It's all very well having a qualified nurse for a mother, but nurses do get a bit bossy, especially after they've retired and have got time on their hands. Dad's still working so my mother decided to start reorganising his vet's surgery. It's absolute chaos. The receptionist is threatening to walk out if my mother moves or interferes with any more of her filing. She means well.' Adam shrugged. 'I hope she finds a cause soon or poor old Dad will have a mass walk out on his hands.'

Tamara recalled her one visit to the rambling Yorkshire house that doubled as his father's surgery. It was as far removed from her own family background as it was possible to be, but she had loved it. Mrs Penrose was a caring woman, whose one ambition in life, after her nursing career, was to get her middle son married off. With two older and two younger brothers, all married, with children, Adam was the only one of her offspring still single, a source of constant challenge to her.

'I know, I'll put some music on.' Adam walked towards a state of the art music centre. 'Something that will create a bit of atmosphere?'

'As there's no tea on the go, I really should be getting back,' Tamara protested, looking at her watch. 'I've mountains of paperwork to catch up on and it's getting to be the busy time of year.'

'Surely you can spare five minutes? Here we are.' Adam selected a track.

Moments later the room was filled with the theme from *Chariots of Fire*.

'Remember this?' Adam asked with a smile.

Tamara let Vangelis's Academy Award winning musical score sweep over her. She supposed if anything it was their song. Tamara and Adam had watched the film one summer's evening when the friends of Adam's they were due to have dinner with had let them down at short notice. Finding they were at a loose end they had returned to the cottage Adam was renting for the summer. He telephoned for a Thai take away and they settled down for a quiet evening in and watched the film, which was showing on a satellite channel.

Tamara had never been able to listen to that particular piece of music since without remembering that summer's evening.

There had always been music channelled into the models' changing rooms whenever they were doing a show, and once when Tamara's relationship with Myles had been at its lowest ebb, the strains of the haunting electronic theme tune had come on air and halted her mid change of costume.

She remembered to her humiliation bursting into tears and having to be comforted by her dresser before she was able to resume her position on the catwalk. It was the only time in her career when she had behaved in anything less than a professional manner.

Tamara's smile was a tad on the shaky side as she asked, 'How are Amy and Joe these days? The friends we were due to have dinner with?' she prompted

Adam when he didn't immediately reply.

He had been looking at her with an expression she was unable to read, but one that sent tingles down her spine.

'They are the proud parents of twin girls and have settled down in a highly fashionable area of Primrose Hill. Joe runs a freelance film agency and Amy practises aromatherapy. She's doing quite well I understand. They have gone totally establishment. Who would have thought it?' Adam raised an eyebrow.

'Who indeed?' Tamara was glad the film track had now finished and she could inject a lighter note into the conversation. 'What happened to the protest marches? Wasn't that the reason we couldn't have dinner with them? Something to do with an emergency meeting of the Student Union?'

'I think their plans to change the world have been put on hold while their girls are growing up. I've got an old picture of them somewhere. Would you like to see it?'

Adam scrabbled around in one of his tea chests and produced a battered album and leafed through it.

'Here they are.'

Tamara took the album from him. Amy and Joe were dressed in traditional student garb of knitted woolly hats, jeans and anoraks. Both were waving garish banners aloft, emblazoned with slogans and appeared to be chanting against some injustice or other.

'They look so young.' Tamara smiled at their faces, full of hope.

'So did you.' Adam's voice was soft in her ear.

'What?' Tamara turned to him in confusion.

Adam tapped another picture further down the page, one Tamara hadn't noticed. It was of her and Adam standing outside her parents' cottage in Cornwall. She was wearing faded summer shorts and a pink T shirt. Her hair was not the groomed style she now favoured, but a frizz of sun-highlighted blonde curls. Her face was covered in freckles and she was busy licking a huge ice cream cornet.

'For goodness sake,' she protested, 'what on earth made you keep such an awful photo?'

'Don't you like it?' Adam took the album from Tamara's unresisting fingers and smiled down at the picture.

'Talk about unsophisticated.'

'That's all part of its charm.'

Adam snapped shut the album and turned to look at her. Tamara backed away.

'Adam,' she put up her hands to ward him off. 'I don't know where this is going, but in case you've got any ideas, I have to tell you, I'm not ready for commitment, and given our history, I don't want to restart anything.'

'Is it Myles?' he asked in a faintly weary voice.

Tamara shook her head. 'He's no longer a part of my life.'

'That's not true, is it? You still meet up with him.'

'Today was the first time I've seen

him in months and we were in the company of his fiancée and her father.'

'Then what are you trying to tell me?'

Tamara took a deep breath. She had hurt Adam badly once and she didn't want to go down that route again. She liked him, but the memory of her affair with Myles was too fresh in her mind for her to consider any romantic liaison at the moment. Her respect for Adam ran too deep for her to hurt him again, but she didn't know how to explain her true feelings. She wasn't sure she fully understood them herself.

'I'd rather our relationship remained that of friends.'

'Nothing more?'

'You do understand, don't you?'

A noise downstairs disturbed them before Adam had a chance to reply.

'Anyone in?' Phyllis's voice trilled up the stairs.

'We're up here,' Adam called out in reply.

'You've no idea of the traffic in town,'

she clumped up the stairs, 'and I didn't get half the things I wanted to. Tamara,' she dropped her shopping and crossing the wooden floor, hugged her warmly. 'I must say the Kent climate appears to agree with you. You don't look half as pasty-faced as a couple of weeks ago and you're filling out.' She cast an approving eye over Tamara's figure. 'You've lost that thin model look. I've no time with diets myself. Hearty stews, that's the stuff I like to cook.'

'It's also why she sucks peppermints,' Adam said with an indulgent look in his great aunt's direction. 'To disguise the onions and garlic. One of Phyllis's stews is enough to set the roof of your mouth on fire for weeks.'

'You must come round one evening and I'll make you one of my specials,' Phyllis insisted. 'We could invite a few of my friends too, couldn't we, Adam?'

'Tammy will always be welcome,' he said with a meaningful look in her direction, 'but I think you'll find she's a bit busy at the moment. Besides early summer is hardly the time for stew.'

'Nonsense,' Phyllis smiled at them both, 'and someone has got to get you two together again.'

'Phyllis,' Adam said, a note of warning in his voice, 'don't interfere.'

Phyllis widened her blue eyes. 'Do I ever?' she demanded.

'Yes.'

'Well if you don't look out,' she wagged a finger at Tamara, 'young Suzie downstairs will be more than willing to step into your shoes.'

'Phyllis,' Adam snapped.

'You're not wearing your sling.' With a mercurial change of subject Phyllis turned her attention back to Adam. 'Darling, was it good news at the doctor's?'

'The best,' Adam replied. 'My shoulder is healing well and as long as I'm careful I should be able to start driving again.'

'I suppose you'll be sending the hire car back then?'

'You suppose right.'

'That's a pity,' Phyllis said, 'I've just got the hang of the gears. By the way, promise you won't explode?'

'No,' Adam said.

Phyllis made a face.

'It was only a tiny scrape outside the supermarket and the man I bumped into was very nice about it. We're having lunch together some time next week. He said he'd see if he had a window. Wasn't that sweet of him?'

'I, er, think I ought to be going.' Sensing a potential scene between the two of them, Tamara picked up her keys off the coffee table.

'Don't forget,' Phyllis called after her, 'if you need an extra pair of hands, I'm still available.'

'I'll see you out,' Adam offered.

'There's no need.'

'Yes there is,' Adam said firmly. 'It's either that or I attempt to throttle Phyllis.'

'There's really no need to be angry with me, Adam. We exchanged details and it's only a very little dent. I'm sure with a bit of touch-up paint, the car hire company won't even notice.'

Adam hurried Tamara downstairs.

'Phyllis's parking doesn't seem to have improved,' she said with a twitch of her lips. The abandoned car had slewed to a halt at an interesting angle.

'I'd rather not look.' Adam's reply was delivered through gritted teeth.

They paused on the cobblestones. 'So do you fancy a drink one evening, as friends? Is that within the terms of our new relationship?' he asked.

'That would be lovely,' Tamara agreed as she unlocked her car door.

'I'll give you a ring sometime.' He paused, 'And as for that other business.'

'What other business?' Tamara echoed faintly.

'The nightly disturbances on your patio?'

Tamara smiled in relief. She had feared Adam was referring to their past. 'I'd almost forgotten about it, and you've convinced me it was nothing more than my over active imagination. I really don't need your help, Adam.'

'You never did, did you?' Adam replied as his lips grazed her cheek in a gentle kiss. 'I'll see you around sometime.'

She watched Adam stroll back indoors. Phyllis was unashamedly peering out of one of the warehouse windows. Tamara waved to her in what she hoped was a suitably casual manner. Phyllis blew her a kiss in return.

Tamara had been surprised at how much it had hurt to turn down Adam's offer of help, but she decided it was better for her to be strong-willed now than to let things start to get serious between them.

Reflecting on the strange events of the day, Tamara drove around Phyllis's badly parked car and headed back towards Bailey's Barn.

Old Friends

'Tammy? Hi,' the cheerful voice greeted her down the line. 'Amy here. Up the revolution,' she chanted in cheerful tones. 'Remember me?'

'Amy?' Tamara's voice rose in disbelief. 'Is it really you?'

'You bet.'

'How lovely to hear from you again after all this time.'

'Joe was on the phone to Adam the other day and he gave us your number. I hope you don't mind.'

'Of course I don't mind. You don't sound a day older.'

'Well, I am and I've gone all respectable.' Tamara could hear the shudder in Amy's voice. 'Can you believe it?'

'No I can't.'

'Happens to us all.'

'So, how are things?'

'The aromatherapy business has taken off big time and Joe's doing well too. He's out chasing a new contract now.'

'That's terrific.'

'I hear you've given up modelling and that you're a woman of business too.'

'Yes. Catering, parties, receptions, that sort of thing.'

'Great. Anyway the reason I called,' Amy went on, 'is to say the boys are bonding at the weekend, and I wondered if you could take a day out of your busy schedule to play catch up?'

'Doing what?' Tamara asked warily. 'I've no intention of joining a protest march.'

'No, you're safe on that one. I'll have the girls with me. We could have a picnic in the park. They're toddling now. I know I'm a biased mother, but they are quite simply the most beautiful girls in the world.'

'I believe you,' Tamara replied.

With her blonde hair and blue eyes

inherited from a Norwegian grand-mother, Amy was a natural beauty, the type of girl who never had a bad hair day or suffered from spots.

'Modelling?' she had reacted to Tamara's suggestion in disgust when her agency had been recruiting. 'I can think of nothing worse. Not for you, for me,' she added tactfully.

The modelling world's loss had been the activists' gain. Every weekend Amy had been off somewhere, chained to a railing or rallying to a cause. She and Joe had met during a candlelit vigil outside one of the foreign embassies and fallen instantly in love. Their backgrounds could not have been more different. Amy's father was a Welsh miner Joe's had been a company director.

'When were you thinking of?' Tamara turned the pages of her diary. 'I'm getting quite booked up.'

'You are turning into a *Billy No Mates*, you know that?' Amy complained. 'What's with the booked up?

Can't you spare one day for an old friend?'

Tamara smiled. She had forgotten how being in Amy's company always lifted her spirits. 'You're right. I need to see those beautiful little girls of yours. Give me the time and place and I'll provide the cheese straws. They are my speciality.'

'So I hear from Adam. He waxed lyrical about them. So next Saturday it is. Ten o'clock sharp. I've told the girls to expect one of Mummy's oldest friends and they don't do disappointment.'

★　★　★

Amy was looking out of the top floor window of their Victorian semi as Tamara drove along looking for a parking space.

'Yoo hoo,' Amy waved at her. 'Hold on, you can have Joe's parking bay. He's moved the car. We'll be right down.'

Moments later the pavement was

filled with Amy, Joe, twin daughters and an over excited dog of indeterminate parentage, all anxious to have a piece of Tamara.

'Darling,' Joe enveloped her in a bear hug that threatened to take her breath away. 'You look fantastic.'

'Get you,' Amy cooed. 'All sophisticated. Move on, Joe, my turn to hug her.'

'Excuse me,' a middle-aged dog walker coughed loudly. 'This is a public thoroughfare. Would you mind making room for other people to use it?'

'I'm so sorry, Madam,' Joe apologised, 'you are quite right. Appalling manners, only we haven't seen our friend here for such a long time. What a lovely dog, Mrs Chambers, isn't it?'

Tamara and Amy had great difficulty not giggling as they watched the woman simper like a teenager as her anger melted away.

'The old charm still works,' he grinned at the girls as Mrs Chambers now all smiles, moved on.

'You know I've seen him use that charm on the crustiest of officials,' Amy confided to Tamara, 'and I've never known him fail. He always gets what he wants.'

'It didn't work with Tammy,' Joe sighed and put a hand to his heart. 'She was the one that got away.'

'Go on with you.' It was Tamara who was now giggling like a teenager. 'You've only ever had eyes for Amy and you know it.'

'Mummy, Daddy,' one of the twins wailed.

'Sorry, darling.' Joe scooped them both up in his arms. 'Girls meet Tammy. Tammy meet Dani,' he held one of the twins forward to deposit a moist kiss on Tamara's cheek, 'and this is Rosie.'

'Aren't they beautiful?' Amy cooed.

A set of chubby fingers had become attached to Tamara's hand and showed no intention of letting go.

'They are indeed,' she said as she looked into identical sets of blue eyes.

'Just like their mother.'

'Now there I agree with you.' Joe planted a kiss on his wife's cheek.

'Shouldn't you be off?' Amy demanded. 'Adam will be waiting for you.'

'Have a great day.' Joe passed his daughters over to Amy. 'See you tomorrow. Want me to give your love to Adam?' he asked Tamara.

'Um, yes,' she replied. 'Where are you going?'

'An old college thing. Probably be as dull as ditchwater.'

'You know you'll have a good time,' Amy chided him.

'Bye, Daddy.' The little girls waved as Joe loped off towards the underground car park.

'That's got rid of him,' Amy turned back to Tamara. 'Look at you,' she said, 'no wonder Adam can't stop talking about you. When's the big day?'

'What big day?' Tamara demanded.

'Did I speak out of turn?' Amy raised her eyebrows. 'I thought the two of you were back together.'

'The last thing I need right now is a man in my life,' Tamara said firmly.

'Did he hurt you that badly?'

'Adam hasn't hurt me at all,' Tamara said, wishing she hadn't protested so vehemently.

'I didn't mean Adam, he's a pussycat. I meant this Myles man.'

'Is there any part of my personal life you're not familiar with?' Tamara asked with a weary sigh.

'I'm only concerned because I care about you,' Amy replied squeezing her arm. 'You know I don't listen to gossip.'

'Sorry,' Tamara apologised. 'I didn't mean to snap. I haven't had the easiest of rides these last few months.'

'It wouldn't have happened if I'd been there to plead your case.' Amy faced Tamara with her hands on her hips, her revolutionary instincts to the fore. 'I'm sorry we lost touch. You clearly can't manage without me. We mustn't let it happen again. OK,' she held up her hands, 'no more questions. Let's get on with the day. The girls had a democratic vote and decided on the park, after a walk along the banks of the canal, didn't you, my angels?'

The twins cheered at this suggestion and with a chubby hand clutching each of hers, Tamara made her way inside the house, to prepare for the picnic.

★ ★ ★

'Would you look at that?' Amy stopped pushing her stroller as her daughters squealed in delight.

'Good morning, ladies.' The uniformed zookeeper tipped his peaked cap at them as he strolled by leading an elephant. 'We're out for a breath of morning air. Mind your feet. Don't want any dainty toes squashed, do we?'

'We certainly don't,' Amy agreed with him as she patted the animal. 'You take care, you hear?' she murmured in one of his large ears, tickling the end of his trunk with her spare hand. 'Come on, girls,' Amy urged after a few moments, semaphoring a message with her eyes to

Tamara. 'Any more of this and they'll want to go to the zoo and I don't like seeing animals in cages. I might be forced to chain myself to something.'

'The park it is,' Tamara agreed with alacrity. Amy was more than capable of staging a demonstration if she sensed an animal injustice. 'And I want first go with the frisbee.'

It had been Tamara's present to the girls and an instant success.

The park was the usual weekend mix of families, fathers and sons flying kites, sunbathing mothers and children play-ing ball games and feeding the ducks. In the background Tamara could hear a military band belting out popular tunes and one or two opera classics.

'We usually sit by the rose garden,' Amy said. 'There are plenty of benches and I can keep an eye on the girls in case they should feel like toddling off.'

After a quick dip into the refresh-ment bag, the girls began playing with the children of some friends Amy had bumped into.

'No worries,' a cheerful Australian au pair had taken charge. 'I'll look after them for you. Nice to meet you, Tammy.' She ushered the little party towards the sand pit. 'We'll be over there if you want us.'

'Great girl, Noelene,' Amy nodded, 'she's doing a European gap year. I'll get the hot chocolate,' she grabbed up her purse, 'with extra marshmallows, and don't give me any of that, 'we can't drink hot chocolate in May', it's tradition. Right?'

'Right,' Tamara nodded seriously, before bursting into laughter.

In the past she and Amy had shared many hot chocolates as they discussed the various crises in their lives.

'Not as good as you made,' Amy declared as she scooped up the last of her marshmallow, 'but it still does the trick.'

The two girls grinned at each other. 'I feel about nineteen again,' Tamara admitted.

'Me too. Do you remember that

night I fooled you into attending what you thought was one of our college meetings?'

'I don't think I'll ever forgive you,' Tamara replied.

'You should have seen the expression on your face when you realised it was a student sit in and I'd locked the door on you so you couldn't get out.'

'I can't even remember what it was about now.'

'Neither can I. You always were a bit of a goody two shoes, weren't you?'

'I suppose I was,' Tamara admitted.

'So,' a shadow flitted across Amy's open face. 'Were the stories true? Are you bankrupt? I'm not dishing the dirt,' she hastened to add. 'I want to help.'

Tamara gave a shaky smile. 'If I'd had you at my side, I don't think any of it would have happened.'

'Too right it wouldn't. What did happen?'

Tamara told her as briefly as possible the details of her relationship with Myles.

'The toerag,' she exclaimed, understanding exactly what her friend wasn't telling her. 'And you say he's been in touch with you again?'

'He wanted to introduce me to Jasmine,' Tamara hedged, 'so we met up at her father's house.'

A frown creased Amy's forehead.

'She's Bob Fenwick's daughter?'

'Have you heard of him?'

'The name's familiar. I used to have a dossier on all those sorts of people, but,' her sweet smile lit up her face, 'since I've had the twins I haven't had time to update it.'

'Don't tell me you're losing your passion,' Tamara teased her.

'Aromatherapy does teach you to use your emotions in a positive way,' Amy admitted, 'so I'm trying to practise what I preach.'

'Good for you.'

'Now where are these famous cheese straws? I am starving.'

'You've just demolished six hot chocolate marshmallows.'

'That was hours ago,' Amy protested, 'and here come the girls. You'd love some of Tammy's cheese straws wouldn't you my angels?'

After an afternoon spent chasing balls, lost dogs, trapped frisbees and rescuing a little boy who had strayed too near the pond, Tamara understood why Amy stayed so slim.

'I am exhausted,' she said as they packed up their paraphernalia, ready for the trek home.

'You're a natural with children,' Amy said.

'Want me to help with their bath time?'

'If you don't have to get back, that would be great.'

A Hostile Visitor

The telephone was ringing as Tamara drove into the forecourt of Bailey's Barn.

'Hello?' she raced indoors and grabbed up the receiver.

'I'm not staying with Adam at the moment.'

Phyllis's voice caught Tamara on the hop. After the drive back from Primrose Hill, she had been expecting it to be Amy checking up on her safe arrival.

'I didn't quite catch that, Phyllis,' Tamara said, wishing Adam's great-aunt had picked another time to make her call. She tended to ramble on a bit and right now Tamara didn't have the time to listen to one of her convoluted conversations.

'After you left Adam's warehouse we had a difference of opinion over that wretched business with the hire car, so

I'm afraid I stormed out. Actually, it's quite nice to be in my own little flat again. Now the burst pipes have been sorted out I can set about redecorating. I thought something along the lines of Bailey's Barn. You don't do home furnishings, do you?' Phyllis paused for breath. 'I'm sorry. I'm not making much sense, am I?'

'Was there something?' Tamara asked, massaging her lower back. She had been treating it with disrespect lately and it was letting her know it was time she booked another appointment with her physio.

'I think I mislaid a memory stick in your bathroom.'

'A memory stick? You mean one you use in a computer?'

'Yes.'

'But you can't use a computer.'

'This one was given to me. It's got some names and addresses on it and I don't want to lose it. I've looked for it everywhere. It's not in Adam's warehouse and it's not in my flat. I think perhaps it might have fallen out of my pocket that day I broke down on your forecourt? Do you remember that day?'

'I'm hardly likely to forget it,' Tamara admitted.

The irony went unnoticed by Phyllis.

'Do you think you could be an angel and look for it when you've got a spare moment? There's no need to post it back or anything like that, just hang onto it until I can get round to collecting it. Could you do that?'

'Yes, all right.'

'What? Yes. All right, I'm coming,' Phyllis called over her shoulder. 'Sorry, darling, I've got to go. One of my gentlemen friends has called round. We're going out to dinner at a new restaurant he's discovered.'

Before Tamara could reply they were disconnected.

It wasn't until the next afternoon that she remembered to make a search for the memory stick. She finally unearthed it behind the pedal bin in the bathroom. Blowing the dust off it, she placed it on the hall table. Goodness knows what Phyllis had been doing with a memory stick in the bathroom, she thought, glad she had given up trying to understand the reason for most of Adam's great-aunt's actions.

Outside she heard the roll of tyres on her forecourt. Looking out of the window, she recognised Jasmine's bright red sports car. The sight filled her with dismay. She had promised to get back to her earlier with estimates and suggestions for the reception, but the visit to Amy had disrupted her work schedule and her work on her costings had lapsed.

She opened the front door and could immediately see by the expression on the other girl's face, that Jasmine was in no mood to compromise or to listen to excuses.

'Hello,' Tamara smiled a greeting, anxious to inject a relaxed note into the meeting. 'Come in. I was just about to put some coffee on.'

'I hope you're not thinking of serving caffeine to my guests,' Jasmine snapped back at her. 'I don't approve of artificial stimulants.'

'Would you like some fresh organic fruit juice?' Tamara suggested, deciding against offering cheese straws to go with the refreshment. Goodness knew what free radicals were lurking in them.

'I've come here to discuss business matters.'

'Then you'd better come in.'

Tamara led Jasmine through to the drawing room, hoping its cool clean décor would help calm her down.

'I have actually been working on your requirements.'

'I've seen little evidence of it,' Jasmine replied. 'I was expecting a confirmation email from you at the very least.'

'I had a busy weekend.'

Jasmine held up a dismissive hand. 'We all have busy lives.'

'Yes, of course,' Tamara replied, wondering what exactly Jasmine did in her busy life and also what the girl would do if she told her she was having second thoughts about taking on her commission as it was proving to be too much hassle.

Although the reception was relatively modest, Tamara suspected it would cause more than enough problems. She hadn't liked to approach any of her regular team regarding help. It would be too embarrassing to have their integrity questioned and she baulked at the idea of asking them to sign confidentiality contracts, which meant she was going to have to deal with this one on her own.

'Actually, I hope you haven't done too much planning,' Jasmine began.

The flicker of hope Tamara felt that Jasmine might want to cancel the booking soon died when she announced, 'I've changed my require-ments completely. I've now decided I want to go for a sit-down meal. I wasn't happy with the colour scheme I decided on, either, and I would like that changed.'

'Silver service?' Tamara wanted to be

sure she had heard the first part of Jasmine's words correctly.

'Yes.'

'My resources don't stretch that far, I'm afraid and,' she pointed out, 'we did agree on a buffet reception.'

'I realise that; only after discussing things with my father we decided something a little more elaborate might be appropriate.'

'What does Myles think about this?'

'He agrees, of course.'

'Won't you run the risk of more people finding out about the ceremony if you have a higher profile reception?'

'I hardly think what goes on someone's plate will constitute a leak in security, do you?' Jasmine asked with a scornful twist to her mouth.

'In that case I must decline the commission.' Tamara was firm in her refusal.

'You don't have the right to do that.'

'I think you'll find I do,' she insisted.

'Didn't you read the small print on the contract you signed?'

'That was only for security clearance.'

'If you'd bothered to turn it over and read what was printed on the back,' Jasmine said with a triumphant smile, 'you would have realised I have reserved the right to change my catering requirements.'

Tamara felt a pang of annoyance over her carelessness. How could she have missed that one? In her time she had signed many contracts and had thought she was wise to most tricks in the book.

'I thought it was a simple arrangement between friends. Was there any need to be quite so legal?'

'It's as well to be businesslike, don't you think?' Jasmine all but crowed.

Tamara realised she had seriously under-estimated the deviousness of Myles's fiancée.

'Surely you'd prefer one of the larger companies to cater for your revised requirements?' Tamara tried to be reasonable.

'I want you to do it,' she insisted.

'Why?'

'For a start Myles has been singing your praises and it sort of keep things in house. Don't you realise this is a one-off chance to promote yourself?'

'How can I do that if I've signed a confidentiality clause?' Tamara asked.

'The guests won't be without influence. If you do a good job I'm sure they'll recommend you to their friends.'

Tamara didn't like to dwell on the consequences if she did a bad job. Myles had probably meant well, but his meddling had now placed Tamara in an impossible situation.

'You don't seem very grateful,' Jasmine grumbled. 'I'm trying to help you get your business off the ground and all you can do is find fault.'

'It isn't that,' Tamara began to explain.

'Myles led me to believe you would welcome help. You made him feel very guilty when your other business collapsed with massive debts.'

If Jasmine had punched her in the

stomach, Tamara could not have been more surprised.

'It wasn't my business,' she protested.

'It was a joint venture, wasn't it?'

'I invested money in it, yes, most of which I lost.'

'There you are, then. Myles is trying to make things up to you.'

Tamara took a deep breath. It was vital she didn't over react and say something she might regret.

'I don't wish to appear ungrateful,' she said carefully, 'and it was very kind of Myles to think of me for the job, but I'm afraid I am going to have to turn it down.'

'What?' Jasmine gaped.

'If your father wants to take the matter further, then I suggest he does.' Tamara stood up. 'Would you like me to show you out?'

If Tamara hadn't been so annoyed, she could almost have laughed at the expression on Jasmine's face. She was willing to believe no-one had ever turned her down before.

'This isn't about the catering, is it?' she spluttered.

'I'm sorry?'

'This is about you and Myles, isn't it?'

'I don't have a relationship with Myles any more. It ended when he met you.'

'And you've never really got over him, have you?' Jasmine sneered.

'I have moved on with my life.'

'I don't believe you. You don't want Myles to get married to me, do you? And if the only way you can stop him is by ruining the plans for his reception then that's what you are prepared to do.'

'That's not true. It's you who wants to change things and I don't have to remind you I hadn't seen or heard from Myles for months until he contacted me. I didn't even know where he was.'

'So you say. How am I to know you haven't been carrying on your affair behind my back?'

'Because we haven't,' Tamara insisted.

Jasmine was now beginning to look

unwell. She had gone very pale and her eyes were glazing over.

'Are you all right?' Tamara asked with a pang of concern.

'You haven't heard the last of this,' Jasmine hissed. 'I can find my own way out, thank you.'

The barn reverberated as Jasmine slammed shut the front door. Tamara sat where she was for a few moments, fighting to catch her breath. Had she really agreed to challenge Bob Fenwick? It had been a stupid thing to do. He was an astute businessman with more resources at his fingertips than she could shake a candle at.

This could be the end of her business, Tamara thought. If that had been Jasmine's aim, then she had succeeded. Surely she didn't still believe Tamara and Myles were attracted to each other?

With shaking hands Tamara decided she needed a dose of caffeine in the shape of a hot mug of coffee. As she passed the hall table she noticed Phyllis's memory stick was not where she had placed it. Suspecting it had fallen to the floor when Jasmine had slammed the door, she got down on her knees and searched around on the floor.

It was nowhere to be found. It had gone missing.

'I Didn't Mean To Hurt You'

The following day passed in a haze. There was no outraged telephone call from Jasmine's father, nor any contact from Myles. Neither, to Tamara's relief, had Phyllis been in touch.

When her reflexes had returned to normal Tamara had searched around again for the memory stick, but there was no trace of it. Her only visitor since she had found it in the bathroom had been Jasmine, but why should she remove it and how on earth was Tamara going to approach the delicate subject of its retrieval? She had absolutely no evidence that Jasmine was responsible for its disappearance.

Deciding that the best therapy would be to get back to work, Tamara baked batches of her savouries and froze them ready for when they would be needed. Her only interruption had been a surprise call from her mother.

'That wasn't a very warm greeting,' Merrill complained as Tamara answered the telephone without much enthusiasm.

'I was expecting another call.'

'Not Adam?'

'No.' Tamara ran floury fingers through her hair then grimaced at her reflection. She really did look most peculiar with bits of pastry all over her face and cheese dangling from her ear. She batted it away. This was not the time to explain to her mother exactly what was bothering her. 'A difficult customer, that's all. Nothing for you to worry about,' she added hastily, in case Merrill should let slip to her father that she was upset about something.

It took very little to inflame Josh's volatile temperament and if he thought his beloved daughter was being threatened, it was a case of act now, think later. Cornwall might be been a long way away, but a little thing like distance would not stop him seeking retribution.

'I thought you'd be pleased to know your father has been nominated for the Golden Rosette.'

'That's brilliant,' Tamara replied, 'what wonderful news. Nominations are rarer than hens' teeth, aren't they?'

'Josh is pretending to be laid back about the whole thing, but I can see he is secretly thrilled to bits.'

'You will make sure he doesn't say something forthright to upset the judges, won't you?' Tamara asked anxiously.

'I'll do my best, but you know your father,' Merrill trilled. 'Diplomacy is not one of his strengths.'

'Which picture was it?'

'That's one of the reasons I'm ringing. It was the portrait he did of you.'

'Me?' Tamara's voice rose in disbelief.

'In his studio. You sat for him last

summer by the open window?'

'I remember. He said my hair was like rusty seaweed. I was quite put out at the time. I think we had words.'

'Well, the committee liked it and it's up for the award. You don't mind, do you?' It was Merrill's turn to sound anxious.

'Why should I mind?'

'There's quite a bit of publicity surrounding the prize. You know your father would never trade on your celebrity status, but some people are beginning to realise exactly who his daughter is and it's creating local excitement.'

'These days I have no celebrity status. My star has well and truly faded, thank goodness,' Tamara said. 'I can't see how a portrait of me would excite curiosity.'

'You'd be surprised. Anyway, I thought I ought to let you know.'

'I'm thrilled for Josh. You will tell him, won't you?'

'Of course. Like I said, he would die

rather than admit it, but he's really rather pleased. He's never been up for an award before.'

'Then it's time his work was recognised.'

'How are things with you?' Merrill asked.

'Jogging along.'

'In other words, don't pry.'

Tamara had never been able to deceive her mother. Merrill could always tell from the tone of her daughter's voice if something was troubling her, even down a telephone line.

'As long as you remember we are always here for you?' Merrill reminded her.

'That was never in doubt,' Tamara smiled.

'Good. Well, you must come down for the award ceremony. You can help keep your father under control.'

'Let me know when it's on. Nothing will keep me away,' Tamara assured her.

Feeling better after the call, Tamara

finished her baking, then caught up with her paperwork. Most of her customers were pleasant and easy to deal with and by the end of the day she was in a better frame of mind. She hoped what had passed between her and Jasmine had been a storm in a teacup. Now they had both had a chance to calm down, Jasmine would realise Tamara was not the right person for the job.

Making a quick supper with the remains of the cheese and some toast, she settled in front of the television, to catch up on world news. It was a habit that had never left her even though Adam was no longer front line reporting.

She awoke with a start. Yawning, she turned off the television set which had been blaring out a reality show. The light was fading from the day and she stood up to pull the curtains. Her hand froze as car headlights flashed up the drive.

Moments later the doorbell rang. It

was at times like this, Tamara wished she had a dog, but until now a pet would not have been appropriate to her lifestyle. As she hesitated what to do, the bell gave another urgent ring. Deciding it was best to face her demons head on, Tamara strode into the hall.

'Who's there?' she called out.

'It's me, Myles,' came the reply.

'What do you want?' Tamara called back.

'I need to talk to you.'

'It's late. Can't you come back in the morning?'

'I want to apologise about Jasmine. She's not with me. I'm on my own. I've brought a bottle of wine as a peace offering. Please,' Myles pleaded. 'I know all about the argument. It wasn't your fault, but I do need to explain why and I can't do it through a closed door.'

Keeping the chain attached, Tamara unlocked the key and peered round. Myles waggled a bottle of Sauvignon

Blanc under her nose. 'Good vintage?' he wheedled.

'Five minutes,' Tamara insisted, 'no more.'

'You're on.'

She unlocked the door.

'I even brought along my own glasses,' Myles explained, producing them from the bag he was carrying.

'In here,' Tamara said and led him into the drawing room.

While she finished pulling the curtains, Myles poured out two glasses of wine and sat down on the sofa. Tamara sat opposite him.

'It's difficult to know where to begin,' he admitted as she waited for an explanation.

'What exactly did Jasmine tell you?'

'That you'd refused to fall in with the changes she had made to her requirements.'

'Does she know you're here now?'

Myles shook his head. 'She hasn't been well today. She's been in bed.'

Tamara felt a pang of anxiety.

'Because of me?'

'No, just one of her tension head-aches. She gets them from time to time. She so wants our wedding to go well, then with the added stress of her father's business commitments — he relies heavily on her for moral support — well, something had to give.'

'Did she speak to her father about the contract?'

'Yes.'

'And?' Tamara hardly dare ask the question.

'He admires what you did. There are not many people who can stand up to his daughter, especially not when they are being threatened with lawsuits and broken contracts, and all that stuff.'

The cool wine eased the tightness in her throat.

'Because of the pressure she's under, Jasmine's been rattling all sorts of cages. I'm afraid to say it was your turn yesterday. I'm sorry, Tams, really.' He put out a hand and squeezed her fingers. 'I'm sure Jasmine would have come with me to apologise, but like I said she's bed bound. We want you to carry on with the catering and to forget all about the waitress service thing. You will do it, won't you? I know I can trust you to do a professional job and it would be one less thing for me to worry about. I haven't had an easy time of it since we got engaged.'

'Are things that bad?' Tamara asked in sympathy.

'You could say that. Jasmine's father bailed me out money wise and I owe him a tremendous debt. It's not easy always being grateful, you know.'

Tamara shifted position. Whatever problems Myles was having, they were his own affair. The wine was making her sleepy and Myles had long overrun his stipulated five minutes.

'As long as there are no counter lawsuits or anything like that, then I agree to do the catering,' Tamara said.

'Great girl. I knew you would. I told Bob we could rely on you. He said you were to have a free rein and he would 'meet all your expenses.'

'Would it be convenient if I telephoned Jasmine tomorrow?'

'Fine. I'll tell her to expect your call.'

'And now you must go. We've both had a long day,' Tamara began.

'Why don't we finish the wine?' Myles held up the bottle. 'There isn't much left and it will help you sleep.'

'I usually fall asleep the moment my head touches the pillow and you shouldn't have any more. You're driving.'

'Just one more glass won't hurt,' he said with a lazy smile. 'And it's nice talking to you again. You know I'm sorry for how things turned out between us.'

'We've been over this before, Myles. There is nothing new to say on the subject.'

'I didn't mean to hurt you.'

'I know,' Tamara said softly, 'it doesn't matter any more.'

'It's just that when I saw Jasmine, all other girls ceased to exist.'

Tamara felt a pang of envy. She believed Myles when he said he hadn't meant to hurt her. He could be self-centred and rather lazy at times, but he wasn't cruel.

'I understand and thank you for putting things right between me and Jasmine. It couldn't have been easy for you coming here tonight.'

'I wanted to come earlier, but I had to run a few errands for Bob, that's why I'm so late.'

'I'll call you a taxi,' she said firmly.

'What about my car?'

'Someone can collect it in the morning.'

'I'll make you some black coffee,' Tamara picked up the empty wine bottle. 'By the time you've drunk it the cab should be here.'

Tamara flicked the switch on the percolator. Soon the kitchen was filled with the fragrant smell of ground coffee. She loaded up a tray and headed back into the living room.

'Here we are, coffee,' she raised her

voice as Myles stared blearily up at her. 'There's the cab now,' she said, as the reflection of headlights carved an arc through the curtains.

'Myles,' Tamara said slowly.

'Mmm?' He put down his coffee cup.

'Do you know anything about a memory stick?'

'Memory stick?' he frowned in confusion. 'Should I?'

'Jasmine didn't mention one at all?'

'Should she have done?'

'No matter. Forget I said anything. Come on. Time to go home.'

A sleepy Myles walked to the door. 'Nice evening,' he said, as she opened it.

'He's a bit tired, that's all,' Tamara called over to the cab. 'It's Ben, isn't it?'

She recognised the driver.

Arm in arm they made their way to the back seat of the vehicle as Ben held the door open for them.

'Love you,' Myles called out as he settled down, 'like a brother,' he added as Tamara leaned inside and did up his seat belt.

'It's all right, Tamara, I know where he lives,' Ben said. 'I'll see him safely home.'

Tamara waved as the cab carefully made its way down the drive.

'Very touching,' a cold voice said behind her.

Tamara spun round and peered into the darkness. A shadowy figure stepped into the pool of spotlight made by the hall light.

'Adam?'

'I thought you said Myles Johnson was no longer a part of your life.'

'Have you been spying on me?'

'I've seen enough to convince me you're more than good friends.'

'That's not true,' Tamara flared up, 'and whatever my relationship is with Myles, it doesn't concern you. Anyway what are you doing here this late at night?'

'I actually came to see if you were being troubled by any more prowlers, but obviously I'm wasting my time.'

In all the confusion Tamara hadn't

noticed a second car drive up. Adam must have seen everything that had passed between her and Myles and drawn his own conclusions.

'That was kind of you. Thank you.'

Adam turned away.

'Adam,' she called out.

'What?'

'Myles no longer figures in my life, not in that way.'

'Then what was he doing here?'

'I can't tell you that.'

'You mean you won't because you can't think up a good enough excuse?'

Never in her life had it been so hard to keep to the clauses of a contract. She was sure Adam wouldn't reveal any of the details of Jasmine and Myles's wedding plans, but if she told him and the news leaked out suspicion would rightly fall on her.

'Please, Adam, don't you believe me?'

'The evidence of my own eyes didn't deceive me. The answer to your question has to be no.'

Tamara listened to the crunch of

gravel under his feet as he strode towards his car. In easing her of one problem, Myles had been innocent in creating another.

Unable to think of anything to say, Tamara watched Adam reverse around Myles's car and drive off into the night.

A Spoken Secret

'You have been mistreating your back.'
Joyce rubbed massage lotion on the
base of Tamara's spine. 'You're all
knotted up and what have you been
doing to your neck?' she tutted. 'It's
locked tight. I can feel the tension
flowing off you.'

'A lot has been happening in my life,
Joyce. It would take too long to tell you
about it.' She groaned.

'We were making such progress too,'
Joyce sounded disappointed. With long
sweeping of her fingers up and down
Tamara's back she worked away at her
spine. 'You must make time for
yourself, Tamara. It won't do your
system any good by abusing it through
overwork.'

'I like my work,' Tamara murmured
into her pillow.

'So do I, but it's necessary to relax

every now and then. Your back is telling you to ease up.'

'I will take things easier,' Tamara promised.

'Good because there is only so much I can do. I can't perform miracles. I need a client's co-operation. Lecture over,' she said briskly.

Tamara relaxed and let Joyce's signature lavender rub sooth away her aches and pains.

After Adam's visit she had spent a sleepless night, thrashing around her bed, until as the first light of dawn began to paint the sky pale pink, she gave up trying. Donning an old pair of shorts and shirt, she had gone out into the garden and dug over the patch of earth she had intended to use as an herb garden.

The work had been tough going but Tamara had ploughed on until the sun was high in the sky. Satisfied with her efforts, she had set about tidying as much of the rest of the garden as she could. It was only when her aching muscles begged for relief that Tamara went indoors for refreshment.

That night she had fallen asleep instantly and the next day she had hardly been able to get out of bed. After a vigorous hot shower, she had made a belated appointment with her physio-therapist.

'Have you been having a fight with a rose bush, too?' Joyce asked, 'Because I have to tell you I think it came out on top. There are scratches all up your arm and look at your fingernails. There's enough engrained dirt under them to start a market garden.'

'I did scrub them, but I couldn't shift all of it.'

'May I suggest your next stop is the beauty parlour? Now, lie there for five minutes while I prepare us a light lunch. No arguments,' Joyce insisted. 'I've got some fresh smoked salmon and some of Len's lettuces and the first new potatoes of the season.'

'Sounds divine.' Tamara was almost asleep as she replied.

★ ★ ★

'At last.' Joyce looked up from the newspaper. 'You've got colour back in your cheeks. How's the back?'

'Brilliant,' Tamara replied, as she finished tying back her hair, 'but I didn't realise I'd been asleep for an hour. You should have woken me earlier.'

'And undone all my good work?' Joyce shook her head. 'You needed the rest and I knew if I let you go home, you would have been out in that garden of yours again, fighting more rose bushes, or cooking up mountains of cheese straws. No,' she said firmly, 'here you were under my control and incommunicado. Now a little later than planned, but lunch on the balcony I think.'

Joyce had laid out the table under a sunshade and while Tamara nibbled at the salmon and drank home-made lemonade, she and Joyce chatted, catching up on the latest gossip while down below them in the market square, the stallholders did a bustling trade.

'I ought to pop down later,' Joyce said. 'They sell the fruit off cheap after about three o'clock and I've got my eye on a pineapple or two. The grandchildren are coming down for the weekend and they always like my fruit salads. Their poor mother doesn't have time for that sort of thing, so I make sure when they visit the grandparents that they get their fair share of fresh fruit and lots of Len's vegetables.'

Joyce was more than Tamara's physiotherapist. Despite the age difference between the two women, a friendship had grown up between them, after Tamara had begun consulting her about her back.

They both liked gardening and cooking and enjoyed the occasional evening together swapping family gossip. Joyce's husband, Len, was a retired engineer and now spent most of his days working on his allotment, leaving Joyce, who wasn't ready to retire, the run of their flat.

Scaling down her week, in order that she and Len could spend quality time together, she now worked two days a week choosing her patients carefully.

'I only kept on with my favourite clients. At my time of life,' she told Tamara, 'you don't want any hassle. Some people can't help being awkward, but I can do without those sorts of difficulties. I like to put my energies into helping people get better, not having silly arguments about trivial things.'

'In that case I'm honoured to be among the chosen few,' Tamara had replied.

'By the way,' Joyce tapped her newspaper as they settled down to lunch. 'I've been reading about Len's last employer, Bob Fenwick.'

'Oh yes?' Tamara felt a twinge of apprehension. 'What about him?'

'It seems his daughter's getting married.'

'What?'

'Steady.' Joyce helped Tamara wipe

up her spilt lemonade.

'What, I mean how do you know?'

'It's in The Observer.' Joyce put on her glasses and scanned the page to find the article. 'Yes. Here it is. *Our roving reporter has been informed that Jasmine Fenwick, daughter of engineering consultant, Bob Fenwick, is due to marry fiancé, Myles Johnson, in the not too distant future in a secret ceremony arranged at short notice. 'No comment,' had been Mr Fenwick's terse response to our editorial desk's courtesy telephone call. Nonetheless, we wish the couple every happiness in their future life together and hope they will grace us with a picture of the happy day.*'

Joyce's smile faded as she took in the shocked expression on Tamara's face.

'I'm so sorry. Myles Johnson was your fiancé, wasn't he? Stupid of me not to have remembered.'

'We were more business partners,' Tamara said in a hollow voice. 'We were never officially engaged.'

'All the same, the news must be a shock for you and here am I blurting it out without a second thought. What must you think of me?'

Tamara shook her head. 'It doesn't matter.'

There was no way she could explain to Joyce that it wasn't the news of Myles's engagement that had shocked her, but the fact it had broken out. Who could have been responsible and would everyone blame her? Jasmine had vouched for her friends and family and apart from them she was the only outsider to be privy to the knowledge. Would she again lose the contract?

A wry smile twisted her lips. Perhaps Jasmine had leaked the news, in an attempt to further discredit Tamara. After all she only had Myles's word for it that Jasmine was sorry for what had passed between them. Adam had misunderstood the reason for their evening drink; Jasmine probably would too.

'Len liked working for Bob Fenwick,' Joyce said. 'He was a very fair employer, but as for that daughter of his. As you know I'm not one to gossip, but your friend, Myles, is going to have his hands full keeping a check on her. Have you met her?'

'It was me who introduced them,' Tamara admitted.

Joyce made another face. 'There I go again, putting my foot in it. Shall we change the subject? What say I make some coffee?'

By the time Joyce returned, Tamara had scanned the article in The Observer. There was very little to go on. She had purposefully left her mobile phone at home as Joyce did not like to be disturbed when she was working, so there was no way Tamara could check if anyone had been trying to get in touch with her. The wedding was only two weeks away and leak or not, it would cause immense disruption to re-schedule again with a new caterer.

'I thought we could finish up with a couple of your famed cheese straws,' Joyce said.

She had quickly reheated them and placed them on a plate.

'You haven't forgotten our Ladies' Club order for the end of the month?' she asked as they both helped themselves to the snack.

'It's all in the diary.'

'Good. The president's been on my back. The trouble is she can't delegate and I think she's a bit annoyed you are my contact, not hers. The garden party is her baby and she likes to be in control. Len's doing all the salad stuff and hopefully there will be a few early strawberries. All we can now hope for is good weather. You will come, won't you, if only to support me and the charity appeal?'

'I'll try to put in an appearance,' Tamara promised.

'Do you know Phyllis Morton?' Joyce asked. 'Goodness, what have I said now?'

'Sorry, I do seem to be a bit clumsy this afternoon,' Tamara laughed as again she mopped up spilled liquid with her napkin. 'Phyllis Morton, did you say?'

'That's right. It seems she has applied for membership.'

'Of your ladies' club?' Tamara repeated in amazement. 'She's a lovely lady, but she'll create havoc. She's very Eastern European in her temperament.'

'Exactly,' Joyce said with a wry smile. 'So you do know her?'

'She's the great aunt of a friend of mine,' Tamara chose her words carefully.

'And a bit exotic for these parts. Someone told me she had an arty background and we all know how touchy that fraternity can be.' Joyce coughed on a crumb of cheese straw as it went down the wrong way. 'There I go again. What is wrong with us this afternoon? You're spilling liquid all over the place like there's no tomorrow and I keep making gaffes. I meant no disrespect to your parents. How are they, by the way?'

'One of my father's paintings has

been nominated for an award, the Golden Rosette.'

'That's wonderful news,' Joyce said with a pleased smile. 'And not before time. Pass on my congratulations when you next speak to him.'

'I will. I must try to get down to see them again, but it's finding the time.'

'I know,' Joyce sympathised. 'Len's mother is always asking us to visit. I just wish she lived a little closer. It means a long motorway drive and then we have to find somewhere to stay over because it wouldn't be fair to ask her to put us up.

'We're talking about taking a whole week for a simple visit. I love her to bits, so I shouldn't grumble and having this conversation with you has tweaked my conscience. I'll get on the telephone to her this evening and fix something up. Now while I'm in efficient mode I think I ought to make another appointment for you. I'll do it right now and no cancelling at the last minute,' Joyce said firmly reaching for the large leather bound diary she liked to use. 'I can fit you in the week after next? Lunch afterwards?'

'Er, yes, that will be fine,' Tamara said, hoping she'd find the time the week before Myles's and Jasmine's wedding.

'You're sure?' Joyce's pen hovered over the date.

'I'm sure,' Tamara said firmly.

There would be only so many of Jasmine's demands her back could take, Tamara decided.

'I'll see you then.' Joyce wrote the appointment down.

'Thank you for the lovely lunch, Joyce.' Tamara stood up. 'I feel so much better after the treatment, too.'

'No need to stay and help with the tidying up,' Joyce insisted. 'I want you to go home and have a restful evening. Read a book or take in a film and absolutely no gardening. Do you understand?'

'Yes, ma'am,' Tamara said and kissed her on the cheek. 'I'll be off now. I want to beat the rush.'

'Hang on.' Joyce grabbed up her shopping bag. 'I'll come down in the lift with you. If I'm going to have a chance with those pineapples I'd better visit the fruit stall now.'

The drive back through the outskirts of the blossom route lifted Tamara's spirits. It had been a warm day and the slanting sun on the cherry trees promised another fine day tomorrow. Mothers were strolling along pushing baby buggies, with toddlers clutching at their skirts. The local school was disgorging its pupils and Tamara was careful to drive through the village of Hayminster, not that she ever exceeded the speed limit, but it was as well not to go too fast at this time of day when the pavements were full of excited youngsters.

Leaving the main road, she trundled down the back way to Bailey's Barn. She wasn't looking forward to confronting Jasmine again about the leak of her wedding arrangements. Tamara hoped she would be believed when she explained she wasn't responsible, but until the real culprit was found, she was on shaky ground.

Her heart skipped a beat as she drove through the gates of Bailey's Barn. Adam Penrose was standing by his new car. After Jasmine Fenwick, he was next on the list of people she didn't want to see. He turned at the sound of her arrival.

Fearing all Joyce's good work on her back would be destroyed in a moment as the tension twisted in her neck, she clambered out of the driving seat.

'To what do I owe this pleasure?' she asked, trying to keep her voice as light as possible and pleasant as possible. There was no point in starting off on the wrong foot.

'Yet again I've come to apologise,' Adam said with a shamefaced smile.

A Strange Confrontation

'I've been waiting here for you all afternoon,' he said. 'I was about to give up all hope of catching you.'

'Why?'

'I need to speak to you. Please, Tammy. I haven't come to make wild accusations about you again, I promise.

'You'd better come inside,' Tamara said, inserting her keys into the lock.

'Here, let me,' Adam offered, relieving her of some of her shopping.

'Don't move,' a foreign voice made them both jump as the door swung open.

Adam yelped as Tamara recoiled and embedded the heel of her shoe in his foot. Tomatoes rolled around the forecourt and were immediately crushed by Adam's swift reaction to the onslaught of Tamara's heels digging into his toes.

'What the blazes is going on?' he demanded hopping around in anguish.

'I said don't move.' The command was repeated.

'Is he another of your boyfriends?' Adam demanded, juggling with a bag of apples before it too split and sent its contents spilling all over the ground. 'Because if he is tell him I come in peace and would he mind not shouting at me. I've got my hands full and there's half a fruit salad squashing about under my feet.'

'For heaven's sake, put the shopping down,' Tamara hissed.

'I'm trying to,' Adam hissed back.

A tall man emerged from the shadow of the hallway, his pale face a mask of suspicion.

'What are you doing here? How many are you?'

'I live here,' Tamara raised her voice, 'as you well know and there are two of us.'

'You know this man?' Adam demanded still rubbing his foot and hanging onto what remained of the tomatoes.

'My name is Pavel.' The man bowed as he introduced himself.

'He's Phyllis's friend. You know, the one who came to collect her car?' Tamara explained to Adam.

'What are you doing in Phyllis's house?' Pavel demanded.

'We've been through all that already,' Tamara spoke slowly and clearly in order for him to understand her. 'Phyllis no longer lives here. What's more important is how did you get in?'

'She gave me key.'

'Then you can give it back,' Tamara responded.

'No.'

'I suggest you do as the lady asks,' Adam said in a quietly controlled voice.

'What if I don't?' Pavel challenged him.

'Then I shall call the police and you will be arrested for housebreaking.'

'No,' Pavel repeated his denial. 'I need clean record with police in order to stay. Phyllis, she help me. You know her?'

'Unfortunately I do,' Adam said in a weary voice. 'I suppose you are another of her lame ducks?'

'What is this lame duck?' Pavel looked confused.

'Never mind, just hand over the key. You have my word, along with that of Miss Cameron's that Phyllis does not live here any more. If you need to speak to her, then I will pass on any messages. She is my great-aunt,' Adam elaborated as Pavel hesitated.

His face lit up. 'Then you are family,' he beamed and before Adam had a chance to realise what was happening, greeted him enthusiastically by embracing him warmly on both cheeks.

Tamara broke into a huge smile at the spectacle of an appalled Adam being subjected to Pavel's embrace.

'You are family, too?' Pavel asked her hopefully.

'Sorry. No, but I am the owner of Bailey's Barn and I would like my key back.' She held out her hand.

Pavel passed it over. 'I am sorry if I frightened you. I have been here all afternoon.'

'You, too?' Adam raised an eyebrow.

'Yes, you were outside so I didn't like to leave. I thought you might be burglar so I stay to protect the contents of the house.'

'Thank you, Pavel,' Tamara said, 'that was very kind of you. Er, why were you visiting in the first place?'

'I need to talk to Phyllis. She give me memory stick.'

'You've got it?' Tamara looked with relief at the little yellow stick Pavel was clutching. 'Where did you find it?'

'Here, on hall table. You had another visitor the day I come. The front door was open. I knew it was meant for me and I didn't want to disturb you so I picked it up and left.'

'Just a minute,' Adam broke in, 'I think that memory stick is Phyllis's property so perhaps we ought to return it to her.'

'No,' Pavel repeated stubbornly, 'it is for me.'

'We don't know that.'

'I do not lie.'

'No-one's saying you do, but we need to verify the facts with Phyllis first.'

'She is helping me get settled in this country. I do little bits of work for her. She give me her old car. You remember?' Pavel turned to Tamara, 'I collected it off the forecourt. It was not a very good car. My friend and I could not get it to work.'

'I could have told you that,' Adam said, 'honestly at times Phyllis is the pits. Why can't she behave like a normal member of the human race?'

'I'm sure she meant well,' Tamara tried to calm him down.

'And I'm sure she sometimes creates havoc on purpose. Look at the day she walked out on you. We had no idea where she was.'

'You told me not to worry about her and you also accused me of wasting your time if I remember rightly,' Tamara couldn't help adding.

'That's not the point.'

'Then what is?'

They were both breathing hard as they confronted each other.

'This memory stick,' Pavel raised his voice in order to interrupt them, 'contains lists, names and address of people who can help me, but the computer I use is no good, so I wanted to ask Phyllis to help me print out a copy or read it for me.'

'You can have it back as soon as I've spoken to Phyllis, I promise.' Adam moved swiftly and before Pavel could object, he pocketed the memory stick.

'Where is she now?' Pavel asked.

'At home I think, in her flat. I haven't seen her for a while.'

'She told me you'd had words about the hire car.'

'I wish Phyllis would stop telling everyone all the intimate details of our life,' Adam reacted with an annoyed frown.

'Can I have her new address?' Pavel asked.

'Why don't you give me yours, then I can pass it on to her?' Adam replied.

'I am staying with a friend. I don't know how long I will be there.' Pavel scribbled something down on a piece of paper. 'Here it is. It's above a furniture store.'

'Thank you. Was there anything else?' Adam asked.

'I will leave now,' Pavel said and drawing on his dignity, apologised to Tamara. 'I am sorry if I gave you a shock, Miss Cameron, Tamara. It was not my intention.'

Tamara shook his hand. 'I hope you get settled,' she said.

'Phyllis will sort something out for me. She is a very reliable person.'

It was as well Pavel was making his way towards the door and missed the incredulous look on Adam's face.

'Reliable and Phyllis do not go in the same sentence,' he murmured out the side of his mouth to Tamara.

Tamara ignored him and asked Pavel, 'How are you getting home? Can I give you a lift anywhere?'

'I walk,' Pavel smiled. 'It is a lovely afternoon. We do not have so much sun where I come from. Thank you. Here are your squashed tomatoes.'

'There's no need, er, thank you,' she said as Pavel shoved what remained of them into her hands.

'Now, I go. Goodbye.'

'I have to get to the kitchen quickly.' Tamara's voice was urgent.

'Did you believe him?' she asked Adam as she hurried towards the sink.

'It sounds like one of Phyllis's escapades,' he admitted as he followed with the rest of her shopping and placed her bags down on the table. 'But she shouldn't have gone round handing out keys to your barn. You'd better get the locks changed in case there's anyone else out there with a key. I'll pay the bill. Until then make sure you lock up carefully before you go to bed.'

Tamara ran some water and deposited the remains of the tomatoes in a bowl. 'Pavel has explained what he was doing here, but you haven't,' she pointed out.

'Any chance of a coffee?' he asked.

'If you make it.' Tamara dried her hands and began unpacking the undamaged items of her shopping.

'Like pineapples, do you?' Adam watched with interest as Tamara tried unsuccessfully to stack two into her fruit rack. Joyce had been unable to resist the market holder's line of sales patter and moments later she found herself the proud owner of four ripe pineapples for the price of two. She had immediately thrust two at Tamara, insisting she take them with her compliments.

'I've been to the market, not that it's any business of yours.'

The smell of percolating coffee distracted her and she instructed Adam as to the whereabouts of cups and saucers.

'I jumped to the wrong conclusion.' Adam stirred his black coffee vigorously after they had sat down.

'Sorry?' Tamara produced a batch of home baked biscuits and broke one into bits as she looked at him.

She wished Adam's eyes weren't quite so deep chocolate brown.

'You know it's much easier reporting from a war zone than apologising to you.' A shamefaced smile tugged at the corner of his mouth. 'I shouldn't have said what I did about you and Myles. I'm sorry.'

'No, you shouldn't,' Tamara replied, determined not to go easy on him. If she kept Adam at arm's length, it would be easier not to fall prey to his easy brand of charm, which she was sure worked well in all the war torn regions of the world.

She had too much emotional baggage to get re-involved with him, at least that was what she was trying to tell her heart. The trouble was it didn't seem to be listening.

'I read the report in The Observer. I didn't realise Myles and Jasmine had set a date.'

'They wanted to keep it a secret. Her father is involved in some business deal and then of course Myles had a lot of adverse publicity when his business failed.'

'Understand,' Adam said and took a large bite out of one of Tamara's biscuits. 'Aren't you having one?'

'I had lunch with Joyce, my physiotherapist,' she explained her own lack of hunger and pushed away her plate, hoping Adam wouldn't ask why she found it necessary to reduce her biscuit to a pile of crumbs.

'Myles asked me to do the catering for his wedding. I was sworn to secrecy, but as everyone now seems to know about it, I don't suppose there's any harm in telling you. Actually, I'll probably get the blame for leaking the story to The Observer,' Tamara admitted.

'Why?' Adam asked.

'Jasmine's father asked me to sign a confidentiality contract. Apparently they didn't trust me to keep quiet about the arrangements.'

'That's a bit of an insult to your integrity, isn't it?' An angry frown scarred Adam's forehead.

'Whatever it was, it didn't work. Someone spilled the beans.'

'Have you spoken to Myles about it?'

'Not yet. I only heard about the story in the newspaper when Joyce read it out to me at lunchtime. I'll probably be off the job again. Honestly, it's been more trouble than it's worth.'

'Again?'

'Jasmine wanted to change all the arrangements. She wanted silver service. When I told her I wasn't prepared to do that, she threatened to sue me for breach of contract. To cut a long story short, I told her to go ahead and sue. It must have been the day Pavel found the memory stick on the hall table. He probably heard us arguing. Anyway, that was why Myles was here the other night. He had persuaded Jasmine to change her mind and I was back on the job again. He brought a bottle of wine to celebrate and I'm afraid he rather overdid the celebration. You drove up just as I was manoeuvring him into Ben's taxi.'

'Where was Jasmine?'

'In bed. She was tired,' Tamara replied. 'What were you doing here that late at night anyway?'

Adam gave another embarrassed smile. 'I was actually on the lookout for prowlers.'

'You what?'

'I didn't like the idea of you being out here on your own and when you mentioned you thought someone had been hanging about up to no good, I thought I'd come and keep an eye on the place.'

'I don't remember asking you to play Sir Galahad on my behalf,' Tamara flared up. 'What were you thinking of?'

'Thank you, Adam, for caring,' he parodied her tone of voice.

'You realise I might have thought you were paparazzi lurking about in the bushes? Or Pavel, or anybody?'

A look of alarm crossed Adam's face. 'You weren't thinking of peppering me with an air gun were you? I'm not terribly fond of getting shot.'

A slow smile moved Tamara's lips. 'I don't have one, but it's no more than you deserve. So far you've managed to disbelieve me on all counts.'

'I suppose you're right,' Adam admitted. 'What say we wipe the slate clean and start again?' he suggested.

'I'm not sure I understand you,' Tamara said with a puzzled frown.

'We could forget about our past history, dotty aunts and ex-fiancés?'

'And?'

'Have some fun?'

'Won't you be going abroad again now your shoulder's healing?'

'Not until the book's finished. So?'

'No more nocturnal visits unless by agreement?'

'Fine by me,' Adam nodded. 'I'll pick

you up later tonight, shall I?'

'Where are we going?'

'A friend of mine's opened a tapas bar, I thought we could try it out.'

'Do you know the owners of all the local eateries in the area?' Tamara demanded, remembering their shared pizza at Giancarlo's.

'Not yet, but I'm working on it. See you later.'

The telephone in the hall began ringing. Tamara picked it up.

'Bye,' she waved at Adam.

'It's Jasmine,' the voice greeted her crisply. 'You're not answering your mobile.'

'I'm sorry,' Tamara began, 'I've been out all day. I only just got in.'

'I know all about you and Myles.' Jasmine didn't bother with any more small talk.

Tamara stiffened. 'I don't understand,' she said slowly.

'I think you do. Ben is a friend of mine and he saw the two of you together.'

'It isn't what you think, Jasmine,' Tamara began to explain.

'I was right about you all along. You are still in love with Myles.'

'That's not true.'

'That's why you spilled the story to the newspapers, isn't it?'

'I was going to call you about that,' Tamara tried again to explain.

'I hope they paid you well for the exclusive because you're going to need every penny you can get.'

'It wasn't me.'

'I don't believe you,' Jasmine said.

'It's true,' Tamara insisted.

'Myles is with you now, isn't he?' Jasmine's voice rose into a high-pitched sob. 'I heard you talking to him.'

'That wasn't Myles.'

'Then where is he?'

A Problem With Myles

Tamara spent what was left of the afternoon wondering what had become of Myles. After Jasmine had calmed down a little, she told Tamara he had driven off after breakfast and she hadn't seen him since.

Tamara had eventually managed to persuade Jasmine that he wasn't with her and if he should get in touch with her she would pass on Jasmine's message for him to call her immediately. According to Jasmine he had missed several important appointments her father had set up for him and Bob Fenwick was seriously displeased.

Soaking in a hot scented bath, Tamara went over the events of the day in her mind.

Who had leaked the details of Jasmine and Myles's forthcoming nuptials to the press she wondered? Unless

Tamara found out, Jasmine would never believe it wasn't her, but Tamara didn't have a clue where to start. The newspaper would protect their sources so she wouldn't get any joy from their editorial desk.

For her part Jasmine had been very guarded about her guest list and even if Tamara had been allowed to see it, she doubted she would have recognised any of the names. From what Myles had indicated, they appeared to be inviting mostly Jasmine's side of the family. His family were fragmented, his parents had divorced when he was a child and Tamara suspected his mother was not likely to travel all the way from Australia for the ceremony.

Tamara squeezed some liquid soap onto her bath sponge, inhaled the scent of fresh fern then trickled it onto her leg. She was glad the business over the memory stick had been sorted out with Pavel and equally glad she hadn't accused Jasmine of being responsible for its disappearance. The situation between the two of them was delicate enough without adding to it.

She was also glad Adam had persuaded Pavel to return the key Phyllis had given him. Tamara wasn't naturally nervous, but it was unsettling to suspect strangers could have easy access to her property.

Although the atmosphere in the bathroom was warm, Tamara shivered. She had put off thinking about Adam until last. She still didn't know where their relationship was going. He had every right not to trust her after what had happened between them in the past but she had to admire his courage for apologising to her for his misunderstanding of the situation between herself and Myles. Many men would try to deflect the blame or misinterpret the facts. Adam had done neither.

Did tonight constitute a date in the traditional sense of the word, or was it be more a case of old friends enjoying a night out? Or even a gesture to back up his apology? Tamara wished she knew.

As far as she could ascertain, apart from Suzie, Adam's neighbour's daughter, there appeared to be no other female in his life, if you didn't count Phyllis. She supposed Adam's journalistic commitments made it difficult for him to establish a steady romantic relationship. He never knew from one day to the next what part of the world he would be in and he could get called away at short notice, hardly a state of affairs to encourage anything long-term.

Clambering out of the bath, Tamara enveloped herself in a huge fluffy towel. Joyce's manipulations earlier in the day had freed up the tension in her neck and eased the pressure on her lower back. Tamara realised she had been stupid to undo all the good work her physio had done and determined to take more care of her body in future. She decided after Jasmine's wedding, if it ever took place, she would take a week out to visit her parents, hear all about the Golden Rosette then lie on a

Cornish beach for the rest of her stay.

Choosing a crisp white blouse to complement the floral skirt she had chosen for her evening out with Adam, Tamara was putting the finishing touches to her hair and make-up when she heard a disturbance in the court-yard outside.

She glanced out of the window. There was no sign of Adam's car. She had left herself plenty of time to get ready for their date and it was still a little on the early side. Hoping it wasn't Pavel making a return visit to ensure Phyllis really didn't still live on the premises, she descended the stairs.

Through the frosted window by the front door she detected the blurred shape of someone hovering by the porch.

'Hello,' she called out, glad she had taken Adam's advice to lock up carefully, in case there were any more key holders to her premises, roaming the countryside.

'Tamara?'

'Myles,' she gasped in relief, recognising his voice. 'What are you doing here?' she unlocked the door. 'I've had Jasmine on the telephone. She's worried sick about you.'

His hair was dishevelled and he didn't look as though he'd slept for days.

'Where have you been?'

'I've done something terrible,' he admitted, clinging onto her door for support.

'You'd better come in.'

They went through to the kitchen. Tamara flicked the switch on her jug kettle and spooned some instant coffee into a mug.

'Have you eaten anything today?' she asked.

'I'm not sure,' Myles frowned in reply, 'but I'm not hungry.'

'Here.' Tamara thrust the mug of coffee into his hands. 'Drink that.'

'Thanks,' he said with a shaky smile. His teeth chattered against the mug. 'Sorry. I shouldn't be bothering you with my problems.'

'No, you shouldn't,' she agreed. 'That's Jasmine's job.'

'I can't.' He shook his head, unable to go on.

'What have you done that's so terrible you can't talk to her?' Tamara asked, feeling a pang of sympathy for him.

Myles would always be a special part of her life, even though he was now engaged to Jasmine. When they had been together, they had spent a lot of time experiencing life and making mistakes that were all part of growing up. The memory of those days would always live with Tamara. She had a lot to thank Myles for. Who knew what might have happened between them if he hadn't fallen in love with Jasmine? Myles had been the first to realise their romance was at an end.

'I leaked the news of our engagement to The Observer,' Myles said in a hoarse voice and through gritted teeth, as if the words pained him.

'It was you?' Tamara reacted in shock as she realised what he had said. 'Why?'

'I'm short of money,' Myles admitted.

'But surely Jasmine's father helped you out?'

'He did, but he also keeps a tight rein on the purse strings. I can't blame him, I suppose, given my track record, but it's not easy working for someone else when you've always been your own boss. I hate being answerable to him.'

Privately Tamara thought Myles had landed on his feet with a future father-in-law who was prepared to overlook his previous lack of business acumen and offer him a steady job. Obviously Myles didn't see it like that.

'Doesn't Jasmine have an allowance?'

'She does, but that's her money. I wouldn't dream of taking any of it.'

Tamara wished Myles had entertained the same financial scruples when she had been pouring money into his business venture before it folded, but she had long since come to terms with the fickleness of Myles's character.

'Well, you've got to tell Jasmine what you've done,' Tamara insisted.

'I thought perhaps if I disappeared for a bit the fuss would die down.'

'Exactly how long did you have in mind?'

'I don't know,' Myles admitted. 'I suppose I panicked when I saw the news in print. Then I didn't know what to do, so I just took off.'

'Well you thought wrong,' Tamara raised her voice. 'You can't go on the run indefinitely and you do realise Jasmine and her father are blaming me for the leak?'

Myles widened his weak blue eyes in shock.

'No, I didn't,' he gulped.

'And if you don't put the record straight, I could be sued under the terms of that contract Bob made me sign.'

'I didn't realise there would be this much trouble. The Observer didn't actually pay me a fortune, either.' The tone of Myles's voice was almost a whinge, as if everything that had happened were Tamara's fault.

'You are going to have to talk things through with Jasmine, especially if you are having second thoughts about getting married.'

'I'm not,' Myles interrupted her. 'I love Jasmine more than life itself. I want to marry her.' Myles spilt more coffee on the worktop than he actually managed to drink. 'Jasmine has always lived on her nerves and I think lately everything's been getting on top of her. We never used to fall out, but recently we've done nothing but. I thought if I bought her a present it might cheer her up. That was when I realised I hardly had any money of my own.'

'Getting married can be a very delicate time for a girl, especially one as sensitive as Jasmine.' Tamara kept her voice gentle.

'I've messed up,' Myles admitted.

Fighting down the urge to shake him by the shoulders and tell him to pull himself together, Tamara glanced surreptitiously at her watch. Adam would be here at any moment and the last thing she wanted was for him to discover Myles Johnson seated at her kitchen table pouring his heart out to her yet again.

'How did you get here?' Tamara asked as she glanced out of the window to see if Adam had arrived. There was no sign of a car on the forecourt.

'I walked down from the main road,' Myles admitted. 'I've been wandering about most of the day.'

'Do you want me to call you a taxi?'

'I was hoping I could stay here.' Myles put out a hand and clasped Tamara's fingers. 'You've always been so strong and understanding.'

Tamara snatched her hand away from his. 'You have to speak to Jasmine,' she spoke slowly and carefully. 'Why don't you call her now? It might be easier to explain things over the telephone, rather than face to face.'

'Do you think so?'

'I do and I know she'll be relieved to know you're safe and well. I'll be in the living room if you need me.'

Tamara slipped out of the door and into the dining room wondering how on earth she had managed to get caught up in another of Myles's human dramas. She paused wondering what she should do while she waited for Myles to make his call.

The decision was taken out of her hands by a flash of colour in the driveway. Taking a deep breath she headed towards the front door. She was not looking forward to explaining to Adam what Myles Johnson was doing here.

'He is here, isn't he?' Jasmine pounced on Tamara the moment she opened the door, her eyes bright with accusation. 'I knew you weren't telling the truth.'

'I was telling the truth.' Tamara was

flattened against the wall as Jasmine shot into the hall, a triumphant look on her face.

'I can hear Myles's voice. You're hiding him in your kitchen.'

'I am not hiding him anywhere. At my suggestion he is telephoning you. He's got something he wants to tell you.'

Not bothering to listen to anything Tamara had to say, Jasmine ran towards the kitchen. Moments later through the crack in the door, Tamara saw Myles throw down his phone and jump up to embrace his fiancée.

All was silence in the kitchen, for which Tamara was glad. She didn't want to have to intervene in a lovers' tiff. A further roll of tyres on the forecourt drew her attention back to the drive. At least with Jasmine on the premises, Adam wouldn't be able to accuse her of still having a liaison with Myles she thought with a wry smile as she went outside to greet him.

'Have you got visitors?' he asked

looking at Jasmine's metallic blue run-around.

'It belongs to Jasmine Fenwick.'

'What's she doing here?'

'She's in the kitchen.'

'Doing what?'

'She's with Myles.'

'He's not here again, is he?'

Standing by his car looking down at her, Tamara couldn't help comparing the two men. They were both of an equal height and when it came to physical looks she supposed there wasn't much to choose between them, but that was where any comparison ended.

Myles would always be the type of man who needed someone to lean on and when things went wrong he would try to lay the blame elsewhere. Adam, she knew, was man enough to shoulder the blame and wasn't afraid to admit he had been wrong.

Adam moved towards Tamara and the next moment his arms were encircling her waist.

225

'Promise me there's nothing between you and Myles Johnson any more?' he murmured in her ear.

'Would it matter to you if there was?'

'I suppose it would. In fact, I would be as jealous as hell.'

'Then I'm almost tempted to say there is,' Tamara admitted.

'He does seem to be here every time I call round.'

'That's not true and you know it.' Tamara made to push him away. He winced from the pressure of her fingers on his shoulders. 'Sorry, I forgot,' she apologised. 'Does it still hurt?'

'The scar aches from time to time,' he admitted, adding with a teasing smile, 'Especially when I've got my arms around an active female. Look, what is all this about Myles and Jasmine? What are they doing here?'

'It's a long story, but basically it was Myles who leaked the engagement story to the press.'

'Myles was responsible? Well, of all the toerags. He would have been prepared to let you take the blame.'

'Myles has explained everything,' Jasmine trilled behind them. 'And I understand the immense pressure he has been under, the poor lamb. I'll explain everything to Daddy for him.'

She was holding a sheepish-looking Myles by the hand. Tamara turned to Adam to see what he would make of the touching little scene. She could tell by the impassive look on his face he was as bemused as Tamara.

'I'll be in touch about the catering requirements later in the week.' Jasmine was now all sweetness and light as she addressed Tamara. It was as if the earlier regrettable scene in her hall had never taken place.

'You still want my services?' Tamara asked.

'Of course.' Jasmine looked surprised by the suggestion. 'Jasmine Fenwick,' she introduced herself to Adam.

'Adam Penrose,' he replied equally politely.

'So you're Adam Penrose,' she arched

her eyebrows. 'Myles has been telling me all about you.'

'I wasn't aware he knew me.'

'Only through Tamara,' Jasmine smiled sweetly at her. 'I know all about how you called him over to discuss your growing feelings for Adam and how you weren't sure where the relationship was going.'

'I did what?' Tamara felt ready to explode.

'We really must be going,' Jasmine insisted. 'Daddy's invited some people around for dinner and they all want to meet Myles.'

Myles hesitated as if he wasn't sure how to take his leave.

'If you take one step towards me,' Tamara ground out at him her eyes flashing dangerously, 'I won't be responsible for my actions.'

'Myles, come along,' Jasmine called over from her car, 'you've wasted enough of your ex-girlfriend's time.'

'Now, there we are in total agreement,' Tamara murmured under her breath.

She felt the firm grip of Adam's hand holding hers as the blue car drove off down the lane.

'I don't know about you,' he smiled at her, 'but I could murder some tapas and I can't wait to hear about where you think our relationship is going.'

A Night To Remember

Music drifted over from the pavilion as Tamara cleared away the last of the plates and glasses. Despite her fears everything had gone well and the reception had been a great success. As Jasmine had predicted, several of the guests had asked for her details and she had run out of the usual supply of business cards she always carried around with her.

In the days following their confrontation at Bailey's Barn, Jasmine had been too tired to make a further fuss about any of the arrangements and to Tamara's relief had left her to make all the final arrangements. Myles had proved a surprising tower of strength and made himself available for all the running around that was needed.

After his full confession to Jasmine and her father where he nobly absolved

Tamara from any of the blame for leaking the story to the press, things calmed down considerably. A responsible reporter from The Observer was given permission to report on the occasion, provided he made no reference to Bob Fenwick's deals, or Myles's past business history.

Myles and Jasmine had exchanged their vows privately in front of only close family at a private service in the local registry office, then the party had moved on to the champagne reception where the rest of their friends were waiting to toast the happy couple in the Jacobean Room of Bob Fenwick's manor house.

Jasmine had chosen to wear a simple white shift and a plain pillbox hat with a veil for the service of blessing in the rose arbour. Her bouquet had been composed of miniature red roses and a silver horseshoe. To Tamara's embarrassment she had been its reluctant recipient as Jasmine deliberately tossed it at her. Tamara hadn't seen it coming.

Along with the invited guests, she had been listening entranced to the simple vows Jasmine and Myles had exchanged, promising to always love, honour, cherish and care for each other. It had been a moving service and catching the bride's bouquet had been the last thought on Tamara's mind. She had buried her nose in the blooms to hide her blushes as the guests broke into a spontaneous round of applause.

As if to make up for all past differences between them, Jasmine had gone through a complete character makeover and on several occasions went the extra mile to ensure Tamara had everything she wanted by way of help.

'I feel guilty,' she confessed over a snatched cup of tea in the kitchen before Jasmine went up to change into her going away outfit, 'for suspecting you of being involved with leaking the story to the press.'

'You weren't to know it wasn't me,' Tamara said.

'It could have been anybody, but I'm sorry I accused you. I also suspect Myles chose to be economical with the truth regarding the real reason for his visits to Bailey's Barn?'

'There really is nothing between us any more,' Tamara insisted, ignoring the invitation to share any confidences of that nature with Jasmine. One false word and they could be back to square one.

'I believe you,' Jasmine said with her sweet smile. 'I'm sorry I was so difficult. You have to understand you were the beautiful ex-girlfriend, the international model. You were clever and accomplished too. When things went pear-shaped and Myles deserted you for me, instead of feeling sorry for yourself you built up another career. I don't know that I could have done that. I also felt bad over the way we treated you. Myles didn't let you down very gently.'

'It's all in the past,' Tamara insisted, wishing Jasmine would change the subject.

'It was on Myles's conscience too. That's why he suggested you do our catering, but when he did, I was jealous. It was an emotion that got the better of me. I wanted to make things as difficult as possible for you. I'm sorry. I behaved badly. I hope you can find it in my heart to forgive me.'

'There's nothing to forgive,' Tamara said, 'and that was quite some apology.'

The two girls smiled at each other. Tamara's trained eye noticed the dark circles under Jasmine's eyes, blemishes that no amount of make-up could disguise. She suspected Jasmine had not been sleeping well and hoped her confession would ease her troubled conscience.

'There's one thing I won't apologise for.' Jasmine tapped the bouquet of red roses that Tamara had placed on the dresser. 'You were a deliberate target.'

Tamara bit her lip. Had she relaxed her guard too soon? Was Jasmine still trying to trap her into a confession?

'I've already explained there is

nothing between Myles and myself apart from an old friendship.'

'I'm referring to Adam, not Myles.'

Tamara knew it wasn't the heat of the day or the hard work that caused the sudden raise in her temperature. She wished she could fan her face with one of the unused paper serviettes, but she didn't want to draw Jasmine's attention to her heightened colour.

'You are in love with him, aren't you?'

Tamara shook her head. 'No, I'm not. Really.'

'I don't believe you.'

'You don't understand.'

'I know the two of you were an item before you started going out with Myles.'

'We weren't even that,' Tamara insisted, wishing she could think of an excuse to go back outside and see if there was anything she could do.

The night out at the tapas bar had not been anything like the romantic rendezvous Tamara had been expecting.

Adam's friend had invited over several other acquaintances from their shared journalistic days and the evening had evolved into a typical media party.

There had been no time for more than a few shared words with Adam before he was whisked away by one of his old crowd, leaving Tamara to spend the evening with Max, the owner of the bar, who regaled her with stories of their days as cub reporters and all the antics they had indulged in before more serious responsibilities took over their lives.

'There you are,' Myles burst into the kitchen, 'I've been looking for you everywhere. I thought you were going upstairs to change hours ago.' He glanced from Jasmine to Tamara, then back to Jasmine again a look of apprehension on his face. 'You haven't been discussing me, have you?'

'You should be so lucky,' Jasmine retaliated. 'Tamara and I have far more important things to discuss.' She stood up. 'Best go and change. You will stay on, won't you, Tamara, not to work but as a guest?'

'I was going to have an early night.'

'Nonsense,' Myles endorsed Jasmine's invitation. 'Your helpers would never forgive you if you passed up the chance for an evening of dancing and music at The Manor House. You've all done an excellent job. Stay and enjoy yourselves. We've invited a few more friends to join us later. I expect there will be one or two faces you recognise.'

Suspecting she might have been blackmailed into accepting their invitation, Tamara watched the happy couple drift upstairs. From the way Myles encircled Jasmine in his arms as if she were a fragile piece of china, she knew they were right for each other.

After passing on the message about the party to her team of assistants and inviting them to refresh themselves on the remains of the smoked salmon and strawberries, Tamara left them enjoying copious amounts of tea to quench their thirst whilst she strolled out onto the lawn for a breath of fresh air.

The garden was now bedecked for an evening devoted to dancing. Fairy lights decorated the patio and waiters wearing striped waistcoats were busy attending to the evening's refreshment.

Gardeners were directing cars towards the temporary car park at the back of the house and Tamara decided to stroll towards the large ornamental pond in the Italian garden. A cool breeze blew off the water and she sat down on one of the benches to take in the beauty of the scene after the frantic activity of the day.

Two mute swans drifted past, graceful and elegant and extremely apt as strains from the overture of *Swan Lake* drifted down from the house. She sipped some of the iced orange juice that had been pressed into her hands by one of the waiters.

'Hello,' a voice behind her disturbed her thoughts. 'Do you mind if I join you?'

'Adam?' she looked up with a frown.

'I didn't know you had been invited.'

She glanced over his shoulder. 'Are you alone?'

Tamara hoped he had come alone and hadn't been talked into gate-crashing the party by his old friends in order to get a story.

'You don't think I'd be here if I hadn't been invited, do you?' He looked affronted and produced a stiff white invitation card out of his pocket.

'*Mr Bob Fenwick,*' he read out, '*and Mrs Jason Delauney invite you to a reception following the wedding of their daughter, Jasmine, to Mr Myles Johnson. RSVP.*' He waved the invitation at her. 'Honestly, Tammy, I thought your opinion of me was higher than that. Do you seriously think I'd do such a thing as gate-crashing?'

'Sorry,' she mumbled. 'Jasmine led me to believe it was exclusively family and friends.'

'It looks like I'm one of the chosen few then, doesn't it?' Adam sat down beside her. 'How did it go?'

'Very well. We've all been invited to stay on. The girls are around somewhere tucking into party leftovers.'

'And you?'

'Me?' Tamara echoed.

'You are staying on, aren't you?'

Tamara blinked. Adam always seemed able to read what she was thinking.

'I was hoping to have an early night.'

'Not on my account, I hope?' He sat down beside her. 'I'm sorry about the other night, at the tapas bar. I had no idea Max had arranged a party.'

'It reminded me of the old days,' Tamara admitted with a smile.

'When the parties went on into the small hours?'

'Running your own business doesn't allow for late nights.' She stifled a yawn, 'I don't do them any more.'

'I must admit they've lost their attraction for me too.'

The live music on the lawn had been replaced by disco music.

'Do you fancy a dance?' Adam asked.

'Later perhaps?' Tamara replied. 'My

240

legs are still aching from running around all afternoon.'

Adam slid an arm around her shoulders. 'Why don't you relax? Rest your back.' It seemed natural for Tamara to rest her head against his neck.

'For a little while,' she murmured.

'Good, because I'm comfortable here too. I'm not planning on going anywhere either.'

'Not even back out into the field?'

'Not with a book to finish.'

'Isn't it finished yet?'

'I'm getting there.' Adam tightened his hold on Tamara's shoulders. 'Don't go to sleep on me,' he shook her gently. 'I really do have the most devastating effect on you, don't I?'

'Sorry,' Tamara snuggled down against him not wanting to move. 'I think exhaustion's kicked in now the strain of arranging Jasmine's reception is over.'

'Know the feeling,' Adam agreed. 'It's always like that after we've done one of our in depth specials.'

The tempo of the music on the lawn slowed and rising towards them on the night air, she heard the strains of *Chariots of Fire*.

'Listen,' Adam nuzzled her ear, 'they're playing our tune. Come on,' he dragged Tamara to her feet. 'I'm a hopeless dancer, but I can shuffle with the best of them. Let's do a quick turn around the ornamental pond.'

'You're going to have to help me out. I'm not sure my feet will support me.'

Emboldened by the surge of electricity the music had created between them, Tamara swayed obediently to the rhythm.

Adam drew her closer into his arms. As he kissed her fireworks lit up the night sky. Rocket after rocket exploded, sending cascades of silver, green and purple sparklers into the air.

'Adam?' Tamara's voice cracked.

'What?' he asked as a thunderous finale drowned out what she had been going to say.

'It doesn't matter,' she shook her

head as the garden went quiet.

In the artificial light created by the fireworks she'd seen a figure coming towards them, a female figure she instantly recognised.

Their intimacy was rudely shattered by the sound of an excited shriek of recognition.

'I thought it was you. I'm home for the summer and I'm available.'

Tamara watched Suzie throw her arms around Adam's neck and kiss him enthusiastically.

'Excuse me,' she mustered what was left of her dignity glad the fireworks had prevented her from revealing the true depth of her feeling for Adam. 'I need an early night.'

'Tamara?'

It wasn't Adam who called out her name in an attempt to detain her as she mounted the steps up to the lawn. It was Myles.

'Come to say goodbye?'

The kiss he bestowed was no more than a chaste peck on the cheek but as

Tamara closed her eyes to respond to Myles's embrace, the last thing she remembered seeing was a furious-faced Adam striding past her. There was no sign of Suzie.

A Return To Cornwall

If Tamara could have put her foot down on the pedal and accelerated harder she would have done so. It was always the same after she'd crossed the River Tamar. She wanted to race back to her parents' stone-walled cottage and feel it envelop her in its homely warmth, but the twisting Cornish roads were no respecters of car suspensions, and Tamara didn't want to risk an accident.

Morenwyn Cottage would wait for her as it had always waited for her over the years. It wasn't about to let her down now. Her cupboard of a bedroom under the eaves would always be there.

Merrill had been delighted to receive her daughter's telephone call.

'What perfect timing, my darling,' she had enthused, 'the judging for the Golden Rosette award is due to take place this week and I need help with

Josh. He's upsetting everyone. Half the organisers aren't speaking to him and he was frightfully rude to one of the reporters. The poor man was only asking in the mildest possibly way about Josh's relationship to you. From Josh's reaction you would think he'd asked for details of his bank account. Come down and see what you can do with him.'

'I'll try my best, but you know as well as I do no-one can reason with Josh if he's feeling artistic.'

'That's a lovely way of describing the irritable old so and so. I suppose it's nerves really, but you know what he's like — fiercely Celtic, no sign of weaknesses are allowed on his patch.'

'Except where you are concerned.'

'Darling, you do say the strangest things,' Merrill laughed, but they both knew what Tamara said was true.

From the day her parents had first met on the beach at St Ives, Josh had seen off all other contenders for the hand of the beautiful Merrill Cardroc.

He had even faced her formidable father, which had been quite a challenge.

At first Garth Cardroc had forbidden Josh to have anything more to do with his daughter, but Josh refused to be intimidated by the fiery Cornishman and had blatantly disobeyed him. Eventually recognising in each other kindred souls, the two men had made up their differences and Garth Cardroc had insisted his daughter accept Josh's proposal of marriage immediately or he wouldn't be responsible for the consequences.

Tamara wound down her window and inhaled the sea air. In the distance the Atlantic shimmered in shades of turquoise and aquamarine. Tamara slid her dark glasses off her head and adjusted them on the bridge of her nose. The vivid Cornish sunshine was too much for her tired eyes and her head was suffering from a deprived night's sleep.

Myles had offered to explain to

Adam that their kiss had been nothing more than a friendly token of affection between old friends, but Tamara had absolutely forbidden him to do any such thing.

The sight of Suzie with her arms around Adam's neck had fuelled her decision. If Adam wanted to behave like a boar then let him get on with it she thought, squashing down her own traitorous feelings of hurt and confusion over Adam's blind acceptance that she and Myles were still attracted to each other. Besides, hadn't Adam told her Suzie wasn't a fixture in his life?

Myles faced Tamara, a look of uncertainty on his face. 'If you're sure? I would hate to cause any further misunderstanding between you.'

'You go and find Jasmine, give her my love and tell her to get in touch the moment you get back from honeymoon. Am I allowed to know where you are going?' Tamara asked.

'Where else but Paris? I've booked us into one of the swankiest palace hotels on the Left Bank.'

'Have a lovely time,' she smiled at Myles. 'You've got a gem of a wife there.'

'I know and thanks, Tamara, for everything. I hope we'll always be friends.'

With one last brush of his lips against her cheek, Myles disappeared into the darkness in search of Jasmine.

Standing alone while the party raved about her was when Tamara remembered she had promised to visit her parents as soon as Myles's wedding was over.

Merrill was waiting for her daughter as Tamara picked her way down the cobble-stoned street towards Morenwyn Cottage. She waved enthusiastically as she spotted her daughter at the top of the hill.

'Careful, my darling,' she called up. 'It's been raining and the stones are slippery. Don't twist your ankle.'

Tamara waved back, wondering how her mother managed to stay looking so young. Marriage to a man like her father would be enough to give anyone wrinkles and grey hair, but dressed in a flowery top and pink skirt, her shining chestnut hair tied back with a matching bow, Merrill looked no older than her daughter.

'What have you been doing to yourself?' Merrill demanded whipping off Tamara's glasses. 'There are dark circles under your eyes and you haven't been eating properly, have you?'

Steadying herself against her mother, as her eyes grew accustomed to the darkness of the cottage after the brilliance of the sunshine outside, Tamara managed a shaky smile.

'I have been working hard,' she admitted, 'but some rest and a dose of sunshine will soon put me back on my feet. Where's Josh?'

'You are going straight upstairs to bed,' Merrill said firmly. 'I've aired the sheets. Everything's all ready. You can speak to your father later. What you need is rest and you are going to get it, now off you go and no arguments. I'll bring you up some tea later.'

Glad to have someone to tell her what to do, Tamara navigated the tortuous staircase up towards the tiny attic room. Easels and discarded canvases lined either side of the stairs amid a jumble of old cleaning rags and paint palettes. Tamara ducked her head and almost fell into her room.

It was no more than a glory hole, but Tamara loved it. Her tiny bed occupied the whole of a far corner and on the window ledge her mother had placed a vase of wild orchids. She sat on her embroidered counterpane and peered out of the tiny window.

The scene over the promontory never changed. The golden sands were dotted with bright beach umbrellas and she could hear the excited sounds of children playing on the sands and the swish of the sea as the surfers rode the waves.

Pulling off her shirt and skirt, she slipped under the fresh lavender smelling sheets and closed her eyes.

Moments later she was fast asleep.

'There you are,' Merrill greeted her when Tamara surfaced several hours later and went in search of her mother.

'Why didn't you wake me earlier?' Tamara was still rubbing her eyes as her mother cleaned her brushes and covered her canvas with an old cloth.

'I looked in on you once or twice, but I didn't want to disturb you and I made the right decision. You look better already. Now, if you're feeling up to it, what say we take a little stroll down to the gallery and see what's going on at the judging ceremony? They should be coming to their decision shortly and your father will want to know immediately. I don't know what we're going to do if he doesn't win. We'll probably have to leave the country for a while,' Merrill joked.

'Where is Josh?' Tamara asked.

'I banished him from going anywhere near the judges. He's painting down in the studio and unless you have a burning desire to see him, I suggest we leave him there until there is an official result.'

'Good idea,' Tamara agreed and linked arms with her mother. 'Do you fancy a cream tea?'

'I couldn't manage another strawberry.' Tamara dabbed delicately at her lips with her linen serviette. 'Did we really eat all that?' she asked a while later.

She looked at the empty plates and depleted pots of jam and the dish of clotted cream that had been scraped clean by two eager spoons.

'I very much fear we did,' Merrill admitted. 'There was a time when I could have managed an extra dollop of cream, but,' Merrill shook her head regretfully and patted at her flat stomach, 'not now.'

'You're still as slender as a lily and don't pretend to be suffering from middle-aged spread,' Tamara chided her. 'Our young waiter nearly fell over himself in his eagerness to get you more hot water. He's absolutely besotted with you as are half the staff here.'

An impish smile curved Merrill's lips. 'They are all lovely young men, aren't they? It's such a shame I can't come more often but Josh will argue with the manager.'

'He argues with everyone.' Tamara glanced at her watch. 'Do you think we can go to the gallery now?'

'All in good time, darling.' Merrill leaned forward. 'Am I permitted to ask about you and Adam?'

Tamara sighed. Her question cast a shadow over the afternoon, but she knew it was an issue that had to be addressed.

'I think I'm in love with him,' she admitted.

Merrill's face lit up. 'That's wonderful.'

'No, it isn't,' Tamara replied.

'Why ever not?'

'He thinks I still have a thing for Myles Johnson.'

Merrill made a noise of disbelief at the back of her throat.

'I know,' Tamara said, 'but he caught Myles and I embracing. It was nothing at all really. It was at their wedding reception. I was wishing him all the best for the future, something like that, but Adam chose to misinterpret it.'

'He'll come round,' Merrill assured her.

'I don't know that I want him to.'

'That's nonsense, darling and you know it and I don't like to say so, but you are at risk of sounding like your father. I can't count the number of people he's vowed never to speak to again.'

'This is different. I let Adam down badly once. I don't think he feels he could ever trust me again and he would be right not to.'

'You don't still love Myles, do you?'

'Of course not. Besides, he is married to Jasmine now.'

'Then there is no problem. Believe me, darling things will come right in the end. They always do.'

As they paid their bill, Tamara wished

she shared her mother's optimism.

The pavement outside the prestigious art gallery where the judging was taking place was a mass of photographers, cameras and reporters with roving microphones, all anxious to have a piece of the action.

'Goodness, what a crush. Who on earth are all these people?'

'I'm not sure I should be here,' Tamara murmured in Merrill's ear. 'This is Josh's day and yours.'

'It's the family's day.'

'Supposing someone recognises me? I wouldn't want to steal Josh's thunder.'

'I don't think anyone could ever do that,' Merrill insisted. 'Now best foot forward and smile.'

★   ★   ★

'What wonderful news.' Phyllis Morton switched off the television and smiled at Adam, 'and didn't Tamara look lovely?'

Adam glanced up from his desk. 'I can't find those notes I made yesterday.

Have you been clearing up?'

'You know I don't dare touch anything and I never clear anything up if I can help it,' Phyllis retaliated with a frown.

'Well they're not here now.'

'Have you had a falling out with Tamara?' Phyllis demanded. 'Is this why you're looking like a bear with a sore head?'

'Of course I haven't.'

'Then if you're still on speaking terms with her why haven't you leapt to the phone to congratulate her and her father on his tremendous achievement? They don't award Gold Rosettes lightly.'

'Because I haven't got the time. I'm dangerously close to my deadline and I haven't got time to spare for a social life.'

Phyllis stood in front of Adam, her hands on her hips, a look of confrontation on her face.

'You have never been a very good liar, Adam. You're exactly like your grandmother. She was no good at it either. You are obviously potty about the girl and something has happened between you. I don't know what it is. It's none of my business anyway, but I'm not prepared to stand by and watch two lovely people waste the best opportunity of their lives because they've had a silly disagreement.'

'Phyllis, butt out.' Adam looked up at her, a flare of anger igniting his eyes.

'No,' she insisted equally as firmly. 'Josh Cameron has won The Golden Rosette for a painting of his daughter and you pretend not to be interested. Whatever excuses you want to give me for not congratulating him or contacting Tamara. I do not believe you.'

'I can't help that. Now if you can't find anything useful to do will you please leave me alone to get on with my work?'

'If I knew Tamara's number in Cornwall, I'd give her a call myself.'

'Thank goodness I had the foresight never to give it to you and it won't do any good poking around amongst my things trying to find it because it's only on my speed dial and you can't work it.'

Phyllis drew herself up to her full height.

'In that case, should you need me, you'll know where to find me.'

'The last time you said that you disappeared off on safari for six months.'

'I intend to redecorate my flat.' She stooped down and picked up a pile of papers that had slid to the floor. 'And here are your wretched notes.' She tossed them onto the table and with a look of withering scorn in her great-nephew's direction, swept down the stairs and out of the building.

'She's Had An Accident'

Pavel rapped on the door to Phyllis's flat. 'Are you in?' he called through the letterbox after a few moments when he received no reply. 'We have a meeting. Remember? You were going to take me to a contact of yours. It's about a job?'

He looked around in frustration. His father had warned him that Phyllis was not the most reliable of people when it came to arrangements. She had let him down on more than one occasion.

'Can you help me, please?' he asked one of her neighbours, collecting his mail from the boxes at the foot of the stairwell.

'Problem?' the man asked.

'Mrs Morton. She is not answering her door.'

'Perhaps she's out?'

'We had an appointment. I don't

want to go all the way home without making sure.'

'There are duplicate sets of keys in the janitor's office. I'll take you over if you like.'

'Phyllis Morton you say?' The janitor squinted at his key cupboard. 'Here we are. Number two. What's the problem?'

'We have made arrangements to meet. I come all the way from London, but there is no reply.'

'I'll try the house phone.'

It rang out for several moments. 'Mmm,' the janitor replaced the receiver. 'No answer. You say you are a friend of hers?'

'Yes,' Pavel nodded. 'She was to help me with a job.'

'That sounds like Phyllis.' He picked up the key and weighed it carefully in his hand. 'It's not something I like doing. The residents have a right to privacy.'

'She lives alone. Suppose something has happened to her?'

The janitor nodded. 'You've got a point there.'

The two men strolled across the forecourt.

'See, light is on.' Pavel pointed to one of Phyllis's windows.

'You're right. Come on,' the janitor urged Pavel.

They unlocked her door.

'Mrs Morton?'

Phyllis groaned in reply.

'Where are you?' Pavel called out.

'The bedroom.'

Ducking under a ladder, he ran down the corridor towards the prone figure on the carpet. Her ankle was twisted at a bad angle and her face was grey with pain.

'What happened?' he demanded.

'Doing a bit of decorating,' she explained through gritted teeth. 'Fell.'

'You stay with her,' the janitor instructed. 'I'll call an ambulance.'

Pavel knelt down beside Phyllis. 'Does it hurt?' he asked putting out a hand.

'Don't touch it,' she yelped.

'How long have you been here?'

'Don't know.' She bit her lip. 'Do you think that ambulance will be long?'

'It will mean an overnight stay, for observation,' the doctor informed Pavel after the injury had been x-rayed. 'The ankle isn't broken, but it is badly bruised and she will need to walk on crutches for a while.'

'I see,' Pavel replied as he struggled to understand all the doctor was telling him. In the confusion, his knowledge of English was deserting him. He wasn't sure what crutches were.

'Are you a relation?'

'No. I am a friend.'

'Could you get a message to her family?'

'Yes,' he replied. 'I try.'

Outside on the pavement, Pavel bit his lip. Adam would be the person to call, but he did not have the number. He pulled out his wallet and a business card fluttered to the ground. Bending to retrieve it, he saw Tamara's name displayed in bold blue lettering. She would be the lady to call.

'Hello?' Tamara answered the telephone as she was going through the pile of letters on her doormat.

She had only just returned from Cornwall. Josh had celebrated winning his award for well over a week and would not hear of his daughter going home until he was partied out.

'You young people have no stamina,' he complained when Tamara first suggested leaving. 'We have lots more partying to do. Everyone wants a piece of us,' Josh boomed out, 'and you need a rest.'

A rest was exactly what Tamara was not getting she had thought ruefully as she prepared for yet another social occasion. She loved Josh and Merrill's friends dearly, but they certainly knew how to party and they did not consider it to be a proper celebration unless dawn was breaking across the sky by the time everyone decided to call it a day. How anyone ever got any work done was beyond her comprehension.

'Mr Ravinoski here.' The voice down

the receiver broke into her thoughts.

'Who?' Tamara frowned into the receiver. 'Are you a friend of Phyllis's?' she asked.

'Yes.'

Tamara's frown cleared. 'She doesn't live here any more. She has moved,' she said slowly and clearly.

'It's Pavel. You remember me?'

Tamara wondered when, if ever, Pavel would understand that it was she who now lived in Bailey's Barn.

'I have message for Adam,' he said before Tamara could speak.

'He doesn't live here either.'

'It is from Phyllis.'

'Why doesn't she call him herself?'

'Do you have number for Adam?'

Tamara was beginning to wish she hadn't answered the call as the doorbell now rang.

'Tamara?' Joyce poked her head around the open door.

'Joyce,' she greeted her physio. 'Have I missed an appointment?'

'No. Thought I'd drop by and see

how you are as I was in the area treating another patient, any tea on the go? Saw you on the news. Congratulations are in order. Well done, Josh. You must all be thrilled to bits.' She put a hand to her mouth. 'Sorry, didn't realise you were on the telephone.'

'Be with you in a minute.' Tamara indicated the kitchen and Joyce hurried on through.

'Hello?' Pavel raised his voice. 'You are there?'

'Yes. Er, what was it exactly you wanted?'

'Adam's telephone number.'

Tamara still wasn't sure why Pavel wanted it.

'Perhaps you would like to call him for me with Phyllis's message?' Pavel suggested. 'My English is not so good.'

'I'm sure you'll manage,' Tamara said firmly.

'You don't want to talk to Adam?'

'Not at the moment.'

A quick trawl of her email inbox had revealed no messages from him and there had been no telephone calls. Adam obviously had no wish to keep in touch.

'Do you have his number? Phyllis did not give it to me.'

'Where are you now?'

'I am using her mobile phone. I need to talk to Adam.'

'You'll find the number on her speed dial,' Tamara said. Reluctant though she was to call Adam herself, she didn't think it would be fair to give out his number to one of Phyllis's needy friends just because he professed to be trying to contact him. 'Just scroll down the numbers.'

'What is this scroll?' Pavel sounded confused.

'Press the buttons until you find it. Look, I really must go. Give my love to Phyllis.'

Pavel was still talking as she replaced the receiver, but she pretended not to hear him.

'Joyce?' she called out as she headed for the kitchen. 'Have you made the tea?'

'Please, you help?' Pavel accosted a passer by and with his help managed to find Adam's number to call.

'Hello,' he said as Adam's answering machine kicked in. 'This is Pavel. Tamara tell me what to do. I am using Phyllis's phone because she is in the hospital. She has had accident. Hope you get this message. Goodbye,' he said as the mobile signal faded and he was cut off.

* * *

'Cooee,' Suzie called up the stairs of the warehouse. 'Adam, are in you in?'

'Up here,' he replied, stifling his annoyance at the further interruption. The telephone had been ringing constantly since he had put it onto record and unexpected callers weren't welcome, 'but I'm busy.'

'Only dropped by to say I'm off to France tomorrow with a friend, so I won't be around for a while.'

'Have a good time,' he said not

looking up from his copy.

'I've finished typing up your notes. Shall I put them here on the table?'

'Thanks.'

'Wasn't it great about your girl-friend's father winning that award?' Suzie arranged them into a neat pile. 'I caught the news item. Lovely picture of her too, wasn't it? Don't you think so?' Suzie asked when she received no reply.

'Hmm,' Adam said.

'You must be so pleased for her. Will you be having a private celebration when she gets back?'

'I don't think so.'

'Better go,' Suzie said hurriedly as Adam's expression darkened. 'Have a good summer.'

Suzie's bluebell perfume lingered on the air after she made her hasty exit. Adam sat where he was for a few moments. The draft of his book was finished, but he had no wish to ring his publishers. All he could think about was Tamara and the last time he had seen her. She had been in Myles's arms and he was kissing her.

He couldn't help wondering what quality Myles possessed that made him so special. Adam looked across to the picture in the newspaper. Tamara and her parents were smiling for the camera. Her father had his arms around his wife and daughter and he was holding the coveted Golden Rosette. They all looked so happy. He knew he should telephone Tamara, but he didn't know how he would react to the sound of her voice.

Unable to concentrate he prowled around the warehouse. He flicked the telephone switch and listened to his messages.

'This is Pavel . . . '

Moments later Adam was hurtling out of the building and on his way to the hospital.

'Miss Cameron?' he rushed up to the reception desk.

'I'm sorry?' the nurse inspected the admissions. 'We don't have anyone of that name checked in. Do you know when she arrived?'

'Not sure, earlier today, I think. She's had an accident.'

'What sort of accident?'

'I don't know that either.'

The nurse shook her head. 'There's no-one here with that name,' she insisted.

'There has to be. I received a call saying she was here.'

'Are you family?'

'No.'

'Then perhaps if you could contact someone who is and they may be able to give you more details?'

'You don't understand.' Adam raised his voice. 'I have to see her.'

'I do understand, sir and please don't shout at me.' She pointed to a notice, advising visitors of the expected standard code of behaviour towards the staff. 'I'm doing my best to help you.'

'All you've done is tell me she's not here.'

'According to my records, she isn't.'

'Then where is she?'

'Until you give me some more information I cannot help you. Now if you don't mind. I am extremely busy, sir.'

Fighting down the urge to lean over the desk and inspect the display himself Adam turned away from the desk and bumped into a figure standing behind him.

'Hello,' Myles smiled at Adam, 'you here too?'

'What are you doing here?'

'I've come to see the patient, of course.'

'I might have guessed she'd contact you when I didn't pick up the call.'

'Sorry?' Myles looked confused.

'I hope you have better luck at the desk then I did, or is she booked in as Mrs Johnson?'

Myles raised his eyebrows. 'Of course she's booked in as my wife.'

'I wouldn't have expected anything less,' Adam all but sneered at him.

'Look I don't know what all this is about,' Myles began.

'Would you mind moving on, please?' the nurse indicated the growing queue behind them.

'Don't worry,' Adam said quietly, 'I'm going. Give her my love, will you?' he said to Myles. 'Tell her I said congratulations.'

'Thank you. I will,' Myles replied.

Too wound up to hear Myles say, 'It's good news, isn't it?' Adam headed for the door.

'What Are You Doing Here?'

Tamara knew the flowerbeds were in dire need of weeding. She inhaled the smell of new mown grass as she sat under her sunshade, sipping a fruit juice. Having spent all morning in her kitchen, she was glad to take the chance to relax for a few moments in the fresh air. The sun shone out of a cloudless blue sky. It was much easier to sit and do absolutely nothing rather than indulge in back breaking activity in a sun-baked flowerbed.

At last her daily routine was returning to something like normal. On her return home from Cornwall the number of congratulatory emails and goodwill messages she had received with regard to Josh's award had surprised her. She had not realised his reputation was so well respected. Tamara's ex-agent had even been in touch and after expressing her congratulations had tried to try to persuade her to return to modelling, but Tamara had declined the offer.

Over the past few weeks she had seen more than enough action to last a lifetime. She swirled the ice round in her glass and watched it melt. She supposed it had all started the day Phyllis crash-landed on her front doorstep. Tamara would have liked to contact Phyllis to see how she was, but there had been no word from her for a while.

Tamara supposed Adam had told her about the incident with Myles at the wedding reception and like Adam, Phyllis had decided she and Myles would continue to pursue their friendship and his marriage to Jasmine would make no difference to the relationship, which was a shame.

Infuriating though Phyllis could be at times, Tamara missed the older woman's company. As for Adam, Tamara stopped swirling her glass. She really didn't want to think about him. After all he had said about Suzie being no more than a friend, Tamara had watched the girl throw herself into his arms and tell him she was available.

Tamara stretched out her legs, leaned back in her sun chair and closed her eyes. She was still catching up on sleep after her Cornish break. A five minute catnap was what she needed before she went back to work.

The buzzing of her mobile phone stirred her from her slumbers. Blinking in the sunshine, Tamara stretched and took a few moments to get her thoughts together before she answered it.

'Hi, it's Myles,' he greeted her. 'Sorry I haven't been in touch before now. Time goes so quickly.'

'Did you have a good time in Paris?' she asked.

'It was wonderful. We did all the touristy things, had a moonlit meal on a bateau mouche, walked round The Louvre until our feet nearly fell off then went up the Eiffel Tower. The views were spectacular.'

'Sounds lovely.'

'Jasmine sends you her love by the way and said she's sorry she can't call you herself.'

'Is she busy?' Tamara asked hoping she hadn't seen Myles kissing her at the reception, misread the situation and taken against her again.

'She's in hospital.'

'What?' Tamara sat up straight.

'No need to be alarmed. It's only a check up.' There was a pause down the line. 'The thing is, at first we thought we'd overdone the sightseeing in Paris. Jasmine was very tired after we got back and you know how stressed out she was with all that business over her father. Anyway I insisted she made an appointment to see her doctor and to cut a very long story short, she is in the early stages of pregnancy and they think it's twins.'

'What?'

'Apparently they run in her father's

family. Of course she's going to have to take things easy, but when we're properly settled, she'd love a visit from you.'

'That's wonderful news.'

'By the way, I bumped into Adam at the hospital when I was visiting Jasmine.'

'What was he doing there?'

'I don't know, but we had a really peculiar conversation about Jasmine. He wanted to know if I'd booked her in as my wife.'

'Come again?'

'I know and it gets ever weirder. Later on I also bumped into that great-aunt of his in the corridor. Phyllis, isn't it?'

'I didn't realise you knew her.'

'I met her once at an arty thing Jasmine dragged me along to. Anyway Phyllis was hobbling around on crutches. Said she'd had a fall and injured her ankle and they were keeping her in for observation. By all events she was driving everyone mad because she wouldn't stay in bed. So that's all my news. I'd better go. Catch up with you again soon.'

As Tamara finished the call her thoughts were in turmoil. Had that been the reason Pavel wanted to contact Adam, to tell him about Phyllis? A pang of guilt stabbed Tamara in the chest as she remembered how dismissive she had been over the telephone. Pavel had needed her help and she hadn't given it.

Swiftly she dialled Phyllis's home telephone number, but there was no reply. The sensible thing to do would be to call Adam, but worried though she was about Phyllis she couldn't bring herself to do it. He had been so quick to misinterpret Myles's gesture of friendship yet she had seen Suzie behave in exactly the same manner towards him.

She got swiftly to her feet. She couldn't sit around and do nothing. There were no afternoon appointments. She would drive to the hospital and see if Phyllis was still there and if she was up to seeing visitors.

'Darling,' Phyllis greeted her from the hospital bed. 'How absolutely lovely to see you and what lovely flowers, fresh from your garden? Much nicer than bought ones.'

Tamara leaned forward and kissed her on the cheek. 'How are you?' she asked, noticing the lines of pain etching her eyes.

'I feel such a fraud. I am fine. I'm not ill at all, but the doctor won't let me go home. Says I'm not up to negotiating steps. I told him I'm up to anything, but he won't listen. Honestly, have you ever heard the like? One hates to be small minded, but he is so young and he's got very earnest ears, rather sweet really. He gets rather annoyed when I won't obey orders.'

'What happened?' Tamara asked determined to find out before Phyllis went off on one of her tangents.

'I was decorating. You remember all that trouble with my burst water pipes?

It left a terrible mess. After the insurance had been sorted out and when I saw what you'd done with Bailey's Barn I decided it was time to follow your example so I got down to it.'

'Didn't you get help?'

'What for? I knew exactly what I wanted and I was doing well then I'm not sure what happened really. I lost my footing coming down off the ladder and the thing collapsed underneath me. The lady downstairs is away so she didn't hear me fall, but I went down with quite a bump. Then when I tried to move I couldn't get up. Luckily I had made an appointment to meet up with Pavel. I heard him ringing the front door bell and tried shouting for help, but it didn't work. Fortunately he had the sense to go and get the janitor and to cut a long story short, here I am, bit battle-scarred, but alive to tell the tale.'

'Phyllis, I'm so sorry.'

'Whatever for?' Her topknot wobbled in surprise. 'It wasn't your fault.'

'Pavel rang me to ask for Adam's number and I wouldn't give it to him.'

'I totally understand, darling. There's no need to apologise. You weren't to know and you had every right to have the hump with me. I have been rather a nuisance over keys and strange callers at the barn, haven't I?'

She squeezed Tamara's hand. 'Now no more nonsense. I'm a grown woman and it was my fault I fell off the ladder. Fact.' She paused. 'Pavel said he got through to Adam eventually anyway, so no harm done. How did you find out I was here? Has Adam been in touch with you?' she asked eagerly.

'It was Myles actually.'

Phyllis's face fell. 'Oh, him. I thought he was married now.'

'He is.'

'Then what's he doing ringing you? Hasn't he got a wife to look after?'

'He said he bumped into you here while he was visiting her.'

'He might have done,' Phyllis said, fiddling with her top sheet and avoiding eye contact with Tamara.

'You may as well know as it will soon be public news. She's pregnant and they think she is having twins.'

Phyllis's face lit up. 'That is good news. I wondered what he was doing prowling about the place. I didn't recognise him at first. Then when he spoke to me I realised who he was. So you're not involved with him any more?'

'I haven't been for ages, despite what Adam may have told you.'

Phyllis's eyes narrowed. 'Adam hasn't told me a thing. I haven't even seen him. I've been too busy decorating. Have the two of you fallen out again?'

'Not really. We just haven't been in touch,' Tamara admitted.

'Honestly, I can't go on inventing excuses to get you back together.'

'What excuses?' Tamara demanded.

'And you needn't think I fell off that wretched ladder on purpose. That really would be a step too far.' A smile stretched Phyllis's face. 'Think I've made a pun. I feel so much better having a visitor. Seriously, darling, do you know what has happened to Adam? Pavel said he found the number on my telephone and left an answer phone message for him, but his command of English isn't that good, and when he's on the phone it comes out all wrong. I do hope Adam understood it. Perhaps you could swallow your pride and call him?' she asked hopefully.

'I want to know what you meant by inventing excuses to get the two of us together again,' Tamara insisted.

Phyllis sighed. 'You can be exceedingly tiresome at times, you know that? Just like Adam. That's why I think you're so right for each other only I can't get the pair of you to understand me.'

'Phyllis, I want to know what you are talking about. As usual I haven't a clue.'

'Situation normal I'd say.' Phyllis fiddled with her headphones. 'By the way, I heard on the hospital radio about Josh winning the Golden Rosette. I must send him something by way of congratulations. What do you suggest?' Phyllis wriggled in excitement, 'I know, I could pay them a visit. Your mother would like that wouldn't she?'

'I'm sure she would. Now confession time.'

Phyllis raised her eyes in exasperation. 'I can see there's no putting you off.' She took a deep breath. 'That day we met at Bailey's Barn?' she began.

'Yes?'

I engineered it all, not the car cracking up on me. That was a bit unfortunate and I hadn't intended that to happen, but when it did I decided to use the situation to best advantage.'

As explanations went there were vast gaps in Phyllis's account of what happened.

'You're going to have to give me more than that,' Tamara insisted.

'What else do you need to know?' Phyllis raised her hand. 'I told Adam I was going shopping, then I drove over to you. Then I wandered off on purpose,' she announced in triumph.

'You did what?' Tamara frowned still not understanding.

'I could hear the old chemistry was still there sparking between you and Adam over the telephone and I wanted to re-ignite it. I mean I know I wasn't around when the two of you were together first time round, but it was obvious you were still mad about him. Why, I can't imagine, but there's no accounting for taste, is there? Adam's mother told me all about your visit up to Yorkshire and how she had high hopes that something would come of it, but nothing did, so when I read all about you in the newspapers and realised you had moved into Bailey's Barn I decided to nudge things along a bit.'

'Phyllis,' Tamara held up a hand, 'can you stop for a moment please?'

'Yes, of course, dear. I mean I know Adam's my great-nephew and all that, but he really is a very nice person. Possibly I'm biased. He can be pig-headed and stubborn at times, I realise that, but it does stop him from being too perfect, doesn't it? He gets the stubbornness from my sister. She was his grandmother you know and I think I ought to tell you that he isn't any good at fibbing either. His face goes red and he mumbles so if you've got any reason to think he's not being honest about anything, just see what colour his face is. It's a dead giveaway.'

'Phyllis.' Tamara raised her voice.

'Yes?'

'Please will you slow down?'

'Sorry, only I'm so pleased to see you again. They put me in this private room because I chattered too much in the main ward, but it's awfully lonely. I haven't seen a soul all morning and they won't let me get out of bed.'

'Adam hasn't been to visit?'

'Didn't I say that?'

'He knows you are here.'

'How?'

'Because Myles saw him in the reception area.'

'How very strange.'

The door opened behind Tamara and Pavel poked his head round.

'I can come in?'

Phyllis waved a hand at him. 'The more the merrier.'

'Hello,' he said shyly to Tamara. 'I bring a few things for your aunt.'

'She isn't my aunt,' Tamara began then decided to let it ride. Pavel was already looking confused.

'Your downstairs neighbour is back and she said you would want a few things,' he said to Phyllis. 'I leave message for Adam, but it was a machine. I don't like talking to machines.'

'Thank you for all you did, Pavel,' Tamara said. 'I'm sorry I didn't realise why you wanted Adam's number. I should have helped you.'

'You will talk to him for me now, please? He may not I think have understood my message.'

'I think that would be an excellent idea,' Phyllis enthused. 'Why don't you go over there now? Tell Adam I really would like to see him and because you're not allowed to use mobile phones in the hospital, I can't contact him from here.'

The two faces were looking hopefully at her.

'Please?' Phyllis pleaded. 'I need him to help me make arrangements for my convalescence. The doctors won't let me go home otherwise and they need the bed.'

If Tamara didn't sympathise with her plight, she might have suspected Phyllis of engineering the whole thing. She nodded.

'You'll go? Now?'

'I'll go, now,' Tamara replied.

'I will keep you company, Phyllis' Pavel pulled out a chair and began talking in an Eastern European language. Phyllis laughed and chattered happily back at him.

Feeling as though they had both forgotten her existence, Tamara quietly left the room. Her stomach churned uneasily as the thought of seeing Adam again, but she had given her promise to Phyllis and there was no way she would break it.

★ ★ ★

There was little traffic on the drive over to Waterman's Wharf and Tamara completed the journey in good time ignoring the relentless churning of her stomach. Mentally rehearsing what she was going to say to Adam as she drove along unsettled her insides even more. If only she could have sent him an email, but that would have been the coward's way out and she had given her promise to Phyllis that she would tell Adam what was going on, face to face.

Tamara tossed back her head. Perhaps this meeting could work to her advantage after all. They needed to clear the air between them.

Whatever suspicions he was entertaining about her and Myles they were totally unfounded and once she had explained everything to Adam, she could go for closure. They would both be free to go their own way. His relationship with Suzie was none of her business and she wished them well.

Tamara saw Adam's car was parked in its designated bay. Parking her own vehicle in the visitors' area, Tamara clambered out. The heat hadn't left the day and she felt at a disadvantage for a challenging interview. She would have liked to go home first to change, but that would have delayed her and Phyllis would have expected her to drive straight over to Waterman's Wharf.

Wiping her hands on a moist tissue Tamara freshened up her neck and reapplied some lipstick then ran a comb through her hair. The results weren't perfect, but they were the best she could do with the limited resources available. Her career in modelling had taught Tamara that good presentation was half the game. Straightening her shoulders in a posture of confidence she locked the car and headed towards

Adam's Waterman's Wharf studio.

'Hello.' Suzie opened the door with a friendly smile. 'On your way up to see Adam?'

'Yes.' Tamara stepped back. Any hopes she might have nurtured that Suzie was no longer a part of his life died.

'I should warn you he's in a very strange mood. He didn't seem in the least interested when I mentioned seeing you on the news.'

'Didn't he?' Tamara bit down the retort that she would have expected nothing less.

'It was your father, wasn't it, who won that award?'

'Yes, it was.'

'I don't know anything about art but well done. I don't know him either, but give him my congratulations, won't you?'

She trundled out with a bulging suitcase. Tamara caught a waft of perfume and noticed she'd had her hair freshly styled and cut.

'Are you going away?' she asked taking in Suzie's smart summer dress and new sandals.

'I've typed my fingers off for Adam and received precious little thanks in return. Men, honestly,' she shrugged her shoulders. 'Still, I suppose he did pay well and now the book is finished I am off for a well-earned holiday in the sunshine with a girlfriend. As usual I've packed too many bikinis.

'Do you know there were times when I wished I'd never said I was available to do his wretched typing in the first place? I suppose I felt sorry for him. Next time I'll know to say no. Byeee.'

With a brief wave she ambled off leaving the door open for Tamara. She hesitated on the doorstep, reluctant to walk in unannounced but there was no sound of activity from inside either of the warehouse studios. If Suzie hadn't told her Adam was in she would have suspected the development of being empty.

'Adam?' she called out and began

mounting the stairs.

As she pushed open the door to his studio he put out a hand and pulled her inside. She stifled a shriek.

'You made me jump,' she gasped in shock. 'Didn't you hear me call out?'

'What are you doing here?' he demanded.

'Suzie let me in,' she explained. 'I did ring the bell.'

'Where's Myles?'

'I've no idea. Why? Do you want to see him?'

'I wouldn't care if I never saw that man again.' He raked cold brown eyes over Tamara. She shivered. 'You don't look as though you've been injured in an accident.'

'That's because I haven't,' she replied in surprise.

'Then why was Myles visiting you in hospital.'

'He wasn't.'

'You're denying you were at the hospital?'

'No, but . . . ' Tamara got no further.

'Don't you care what you're doing to Jasmine?'

'I'm not doing anything to her.'

'You're seeing her husband behind her back.'

'I am not.' Tamara's voice rose in anger.

'Then what was he doing kissing you in the rose garden?'

'It's none of your business.'

'Then I'm making it my business. The man virtually bankrupted you with his business scheme. He left you in the lurch for another woman. He's treated you badly and you're still in love with him, so much so that neither of you are going to let a little thing like his marriage to another woman stand in your way.'

Adam was breathing heavily as he faced Tamara. If she hadn't been so sure that he held her in contempt she would have thought there was the spark of another emotion in his eyes.

'Nothing to say?' he taunted her.

'I've plenty to say.'

'I can't wait to hear it. Jasmine Fenwick may be a spoilt madam, but she doesn't deserve to be treated like this.'

'If you would let me have my say?' Tamara butted in, stopping Adam mid-flow.

'I haven't finished.'

'I don't care. It's time I exercised my human rights in this exchange. They are something you know all about, aren't they?'

'Go on then,' Adam muttered with a reluctant nod of his head. 'I can't wait to hear your story.'

'For a start, the reason I am here may come as a shock to you, but Phyllis has had an accident. She fell off a ladder redecorating her bedroom.'

'What?' Adam paled.

'I had intended breaking the news to you gently, but you didn't give me a chance.'

'Is she OK?'

'She's a bit bruised and battered and she'll be on crutches for a while as she twisted her ankle badly. Pavel found her and called for an ambulance. Then he contacted me and asked for your telephone number. I didn't give it to him because I didn't realise why he wanted it. Eventually he found it on Phyllis's mobile phone. He said he left a message for you. When I realised what had happened I went to see Phyllis in the hospital. She is worried because you haven't been to visit her and she asked me to come over and explain things to you in case you hadn't understood Pavel's message. Obviously you haven't because Myles said . . . '

'I wondered how long it would be before his name was mentioned.'

'Myles said you were rambling in the reception area and that you accused him of all sorts of things when all he wanted to do was visit Jasmine who's expecting twins, by the way. That's why he was there visiting his wife. Why were you there?'

'Because Pavel left me a message

saying you had been injured in an accident.'

'What?'

'Why else do you think I was behaving so badly in the reception area?'

'I don't know,' Tamara replied in a faint voice.

Before she had a chance to move Adam crushed her body to his in an embrace that left her gasping for breath. She pushed him away.

'Adam,' she struggled, 'what are you doing?'

'Something I've wanted to do ever since you walked back into my life.'

Tamara's heart beat against Adam's.

'Why?' she asked in a hoarse voice.

'Ever since I got Pavel's message I have been going frantic with worry. I lost it at the hospital when they told me you weren't booked in and that there was no record of you. That was when my imagination kicked into overdrive. When Myles turned up I began to suspect that you had been with him and that somehow they had thought you were his wife and registered you as Mrs Johnson.'

'Why should they do that? You're not making sense.'

'I don't know. I wasn't thinking straight. After I caught him kissing you at the reception, I didn't know what to do. It was like history repeating itself. You left me once for him and I could see it happening all over again.'

'What about you and Suzie?' Tamara demanded. 'I saw her throwing her arms around your neck and saying she was available.'

Adam raised an eyebrow, the suggestion of a smile tugging at the corner of his mouth. 'That's exactly what she was — available.'

'And you've got the nerve to throw all sorts of wild accusations at me just because Myles was saying goodbye before he went off on his honeymoon. Talk about double standards. Are you sure that bullet in your shoulder didn't ricochet into your brain?'

'Suzie was available,' Adam paused, 'to type up my manuscript for me and that's what she has done.' He pointed to a parcelled manuscript on his desk. 'There's the evidence all ready to be mailed to my publisher. I admit the timing of her announcement was a little unfortunate, but Suzie's a very tactile girl. She acts first and thinks afterwards.'

'Suzie was available to do your typing?' Tamara echoed in disbelief.

'So I think you owe me an apology.'

'What for?' Tamara snapped back at him, still smarting from his accusations about her and Myles.

'For suggesting,' Adam paused, 'actually I'm not sure what you were suggesting.'

'And I'm not sure I want to hear any more of your wild suspicions about Myles. He's over the moon about Jasmine's pregnancy.'

'Were you jealous?' Adam asked, 'of Suzie?'

'Of course not.' Tamara's protestation

sounded unconvincing even to her own ears. 'Why should I be?'

'No reason. All she did was take up a job offer you originally refused, if you can remember back that far.'

Tamara's heartbeat was so rapid now she had difficulty controlling her breathing. Adam was standing very close to her. She could almost feel his face touching hers. She swayed. He put out an arm to steady her. She wasn't sure what had happened between them or when the relationship had shifted to one of deeper emotion, but she realised now Myles had never been the man for her and that was why she was so pleased he was happily married to Jasmine and looking forward to impending fatherhood.

'Why did you storm off after Suzie arrived at the party?' Adam asked in a soft voice.

'I didn't storm off.' Tamara made a valiant show of defending her pride.

'Yes you did.'

Tamara blinked. Her head was

buzzing and there was so much they had to say to each other, she didn't know where to start.

'I suppose you wouldn't kiss me again?' she asked.

'Give me one good reason.'

'Because I'm in love with you. Is that a good enough reason?'

'And if I ask you to marry me will you turn me down like you did last time?' Adam asked, a rough tone to his voice.

'You could always try,' Tamara said wondering why she couldn't stop smiling at him. 'Do you love me enough to propose again?'

'Not sure I do,' Adam's reply was indistinct and Tamara had to lean towards him to hear what he was saying.

'I think I ought to tell you Phyllis said you always mumble when you're trying to fib.'

'What?' Adam frowned in confusion.

'You're mumbling now and you've gone red. That's something else Phyllis said you would do. Talking of Phyllis,' Tamara steadied her hands against Adam's chest.

'Do we have to?'

'Don't you think we ought to be making arrangements to visit her?'

'Later,' Adam said, 'right now I have other plans in mind.'

'Such as?'

'Asking you to marry me. If you say yes, I might even be persuaded to kiss you again.'

Tamara looked into Adam's brown eyes, now soft with the warmth of his love for her.

'Then my answer's yes,' Tamara replied softly as she waited for Adam's lips to descend on hers.

THE END

We do hope that you have enjoyed reading this large print book.

Did you know that all of our titles are available for purchase?

We publish a wide range of high quality large print books including:
Romances, Mysteries, Classics
General Fiction
Non Fiction and Westerns

Special interest titles available in large print are:
The Little Oxford Dictionary
Music Book, Song Book
Hymn Book, Service Book

Also available from us courtesy of Oxford University Press:
Young Readers' Dictionary
(large print edition)
Young Readers' Thesaurus
(large print edition)

For further information or a free brochure, please contact us at:
Ulverscroft Large Print Books Ltd.,
The Green, Bradgate Road, Anstey,
Leicester, LE7 7FU, England.
Tel: (00 44) **0116 236 4325**
Fax: (00 44) **0116 234 0205**

HEARTS IN EXILE

Catriona McCuaig

Two teachers are evacuated from Coventry to the Welsh countryside, where they struggle with wartime hardship as they help their pupils adjust to a different way of life. Will love follow them there? Vivacious Tansy sees marriage as a way to escape her impoverished background, while shy Dinah just wants to find someone to love. She falls for handsome Emlyn, but the young Welshman is equally reserved. How will they ever get together?